COVERT AFFAIRS

SEALS OF SHADOW FORCE: SPY DIVISION,
BOOK 4

MISTY EVANS

Beach
Path
Publishing

Covert Affairs, SEALs of Shadow Force: Spy Division, Book 4

©2022 Misty Evans

Print ISBN: 978-1-948686-77-8

Cover Art by Fanderclai Design www.fanderclai.com

Formatting by Beach Path Publishing, LLC

ONE

Dunlin *Federal Maximum Security Prison - Black Site*

"YOU MUST HAVE PULLED some big strings to get in here." Dr. Genevieve Montgomery, devoid of makeup and dressed in a drab gray prison uniform, looked as though she had aged ten years since Beatrice had last seen her. Her once long, silky hair had been buzzed off, her previously perfect nails were chewed down to the quick. "You have bigger balls than I believed."

Beatrice's skin prickled, feeling the eyes of the prison on her. The clock was ticking as she considered what to say to her former NSA psychologist. "I'll make this fast. You want out of here and I can make that happen."

Even though her hard brown eyes showed no emotion,

the doctor seemed to zero in on Beatrice a bit more. Reading her. Analyzing.

The head of Shadow Force International knew that the highly intelligent psychologist was walking through her mind palace, searching for something to understand why Beatrice was there. Checking behind doors, investigating corners.

Beatrice wondered if she'd had to erect new sections, using her imagination to fill them with trees, waterfalls, and birds. The good doctor had always been able to separate ugly reality into something more palpable in order to keep her own mental health strong and fortified. She had compartments inside of compartments in her brain. "If you're here about Berlin and what happened that night—"

Beatrice leaned forward slightly, allowing her own eyes to reveal that she had Genevieve's best interests at heart. "You don't belong here. Your talents are being wasted, and while I get your reasons for staying mute on what happened, I don't believe the reports."

Nothing about the woman changed. She was the ultimate statue, showing no emotion. Totally detached.

At NSA, she had needed to be that way in order to deal with the patients she counseled. She'd been so good at her job; Homeland had insisted she be loaned out to the CIA and then to the military. Her patients ranged from SEALs and undercover agents to the President. She'd become a repository of covert identities, field operations, and secrets. That's why she was an expert at compartmentalizing, including the situations in her own life.

"My freedom in exchange for what?" The coffee

colored eyes subtly scrutinized Beatrice's face. Evaluating the mask she wore. "Nothing comes without a price."

She tried to remain an open book—not easy to do when she, herself, was always guarded. "I need you." She wasn't used to saying those words. Even though the watch on her wrist was silent as the seconds passed, her ears seemed to ring with the *tick tick tick* of the second hand. Her five minutes we're now down to three. "Here's what I'm offering—I'll get you out of here tonight. My only request is that you give me fifteen minutes of your freedom in return."

The eyes narrowed at the corners. "You can't break me out of a maximum security prison."

Two and a half minutes. "Who said it was a jailbreak?"

Genevieve's lips firmed. "The only way I'm getting out of here is in a body bag."

Beatrice smiled. "No one has ever broken out of this place. I'd be a fool to try it, and you'd be a fool to accept such an offer."

"Is that what you told Mick Ranger before you rescued him?"

Tick tick tick. How did Vivi know about Ranger? Someone was feeding her intel through her iron bars. "Do we have a deal? I give you my word, all I want is fifteen minutes."

"A deal that's too good to be true?" She took a slow breath, as if sensing Beatrice was in a hurry and wanting to antagonize her. "Why should I accept?"

"You obviously know what I can do, what strings I can pull, the favors I can call in. You have a choice—stay here and rot, or take a risk and go see a waterfall for real again. I'll even make sure you get your pet birds back."

Genevieve's gaze darted toward the camera in the corner. Her fingers twitched. It was the mention of her beloved pets that finally got a response. "I leave these walls and I become a target."

She was down to a minute. "I won't lie and say that isn't true, but as you can see, I've made the target on my back extremely small and hard to hit. I will do the same for you."

Keys jangled on the other side of the door. The guard stuck one in the lock, the metal grinding. The briefest of emotions once more crossed Vivi's face—fear, dismay. "I can't." Her voice was barely above a whisper. "If they find out you helped me, you know what my freedom will cost not only me, but you and everyone you love."

She stood as the female guard entered and announced, "Time's up."

"Midnight." Beatrice tapped a finger on the table once. "Don't ever worry about me and mine. Do what's best for you, Holmes."

Vivi flinched at the nickname. As the guard led her away, her leg cuffs rattled. She tossed a glance over her shoulder.

Beatrice winked at her. *Be ready*, she mouthed. *Midnight.*

Leaving a few minutes later, after crossing through dozens of doors and checkpoints, Beatrice breathed a sigh of relief. The autumn air was crisp and cool, nothing like that of the despair and demoralizing lockup behind her.

Cal put the nondescript sedan into reverse and backed out of the parking lot. "Did she go for it?"

Her husband's words held more tension than she'd anticipated. She stuck her nails under the edge of the carefully constructed and lifelike mask she wore, peeling it from her skin. Another sigh of relief.

Tossing it into backseat, she then worked a few of the bobby pins loose from her wig. That followed the mask and she scratched her head. "Once she calculates the odds of her survival in there"—she pointed at the looming building—"versus those of owing me a favor, she'll make the right decision."

"She saw through your disguise?"

"She's the one who helped me build it. Her mother once worked in Hollywood on film sets and taught her how to create them. I hated doing undercover work, and not just because the wigs make my scalp itch. NSA needed my photographic memory, so I did it. The aftermath..." She shuddered. "She used her Trident Therapy to help me put those awful memories and experiences in a box and close it up. Taught dozens of us—military and spies—how to do it."

Cal was two hundred pounds of solid former SEAL. Sunlight reflected off his hair, and he lowered his sunglasses to glance at her. Doubt shone in his eyes. "A therapist and a makeup artist?"

Those piercing blue peepers got her every time, even after all these years. When he returned his focus to the road, she continued to stare at him, grateful they were together after all they'd been through. No one understood her the way he did. No one ever would. "Her disguises were good, but her therapy? She's the best to ever pass through NSA's halls. Her IQ is higher than mine, and she holds state secrets I wouldn't touch with a hundred foot pole. I have to get her out of there, Cal. She deserves better. Her freedom."

"You don't believe she's a traitor?"

"Not on your life."

The highway was empty in this location. The leaves on the trees had turned dull shades of brown, as if the hopelessness inside the prison had leached all color from them. "You're sure the deal with AG Valupa will fly?" he asked.

Yuanita Valupa owed Beatrice. Big time. "The attorney general will get what she wants—a handsome bodyguard posing as her boyfriend for the ball next week —and so will I. There won't be any blowback on us, I promise. The deal is solid. We'll kill Vivi, take her out right under their noses, and Valupa will make sure it's all put to rest. When we prove Vivi's innocent, she'll handle bringing the evidence to the President."

"Have you explained to the Rock Stars what one of them will be doing for our illustrious AG?"

He wasn't only her husband—he was head of the SFI paramilitary teams as well as handing out bodyguard assignments. Beatrice reached over and gave his thigh a squeeze, a touch that promised she would be willing to make a deal with him as well—this one to be fulfilled in the bedroom. "I prefer you to handle that. They are *your* men, after all. Isn't that what you keep insisting every time I have an assignment for one of your teams?"

He laughed dryly, and caught her hand before it slid to

a more vulnerable spot. "Really? That's the best you've got? You're going to dump this in my lap, when you know every single SEAL I've got worships the ground you walk on?"

The *No Trespassing* sign boldly displayed on the outside barbed wire fence faded in her side mirror. *Objects in the mirror may be closer than they appear.* She prayed a federal prison wasn't in her future, or his. "As do you, if I recall," she said giving him a cocky grin.

"You're incorrigible."

"But accurate."

A few miles down the road, Cal pulled off the highway where a BMW sport vehicle idled. Mick Ranger sat inside, reflective aviators on the end of his nose. "Are we on?" he grumbled before they'd even climbed in.

Beatrice slid close to Cal in the backseat. "Midnight, affirmative." *At least, I hope so.*

Mick, who'd been undercover in Colorado until a few hours ago, looked like a mountain man. His hair was down to his shoulders and his black beard was thick and bristly. His normal lighthearted self seemed to be buried under that persona.

At least he'd showered. He sped them away, kicking up gravel, probably ready to get home and see his wife, Cassandra, Shadow Force's Chief Operating Officer, before he returned to this site in a few hours.

He turned up his heavy metal playlist, no doubt thinking about Vivi's exfiltration plan. He was in charge of this mission, since, out of those on the SFI paramilitary teams, he had the most experience. Like all the others who worked for her, he turned inward before a big mission, reviewing it over and over in his mind, looking for potential problems and solutions to any that might pop up. Undercover operatives had their own version of Vivi's mind palace.

His need for privacy worked for her, especially when Cal pressed the button to make the black divider between them rise. "About that raw deal you're dumping in my lap..."

She snuggled against his side, needing to feel the beat of his heart to remind her they were free, not stuck in a black site like the one they'd just left—or worse, six feet under. They'd both walked that thin line between freedom and what Vivi now lived more than once.

"How about I sweeten the pot?" She teased his lips with hers and climbed onto his lap. "I'll make it worth your while."

He growled low in his throat and grabbed her by the hips, tugging her closer to feel his growing erection. They had so little time alone these days. He nibbled her ear. "You owe me, boss lady."

That was one debt she was happy to pay. "I do offer an excellent benefit package."

He chuckled against her mouth. "Then it's time to settle up."

TWO

The slot in the door of her six-by-eight cell used to deliver meals slid open ten minutes after lights-out. A slender book fell inside before the crack closed once more.

For several breaths, she stared at the volume lying so innocently on the concrete floor. The single, naked bulb overhead was dark, but the dull glow of the prison's lighting system sent bars of sickly yellow across her floor, one slim shaft highlighting it. The cover was worn, one corner bent, and the binding creased. The front showed two men struggling on the edge of a cliff with a waterfall behind them. She didn't need to read the title to know what it said.

The Final Problem.

Sherlock Holmes, her favorite fictional character. While he might be imaginary, he'd taught her more about solving problems than most of her glorified education.

That story was meant as a message; Beatrice loved

irony. Of course she'd pick the plot where Holmes died. At least until Conan Doyle resurrected his character to pacify enraged fans.

Would this prison break be her final problem? Would she die trying to leave this god-awful place?

Vivi scratched her neck. There was no collar there, no chains around her wrists or ankles—at the moment—yet, she felt like a caged dog. The government wanted what was in her head. What had happened that night in Berlin. They assumed they knew, and had labeled her a traitor. If they couldn't uncover the details, figure out how vulnerable they were because of her, she was worth nothing more to them than this.

In the wrong hands, the intel in her mind palace could bring down the United States.

For the past long, lonely six months, she could have been helping people, operatives and those dealing with extremely sensitive matters. Those with PTSD and other career-based issues. But no, they'd stuck her here. Out of sight, out of mind, until she'd lose hers.

That's what happened to folks who committed treason against their country. Who didn't cooperate when caught and interrogated.

If they decided she was too much of a liability, she'd never stand a chance against whatever assassin they sent for her. She was a sitting duck.

But breaking out of here? *Impossible.*

Unless...

She slid off the flimsy, stinky mattress and toed the corner of the book. Something had been wedged inside the pages.

When she stepped lightly on the binding, it didn't explode or leak gas, like in the old TV shows. A crazy thought, but Command & Control, the elite directorate inside NSA that didn't exist on paper, was capable of such Mission Impossible theatrics. Beatrice probably was, too.

Bending down, she gave it a sniff. Nothing out of the ordinary; it simply smelled like an old book that had sat on a library shelf for too long.

A glance through the bars assured her no one was outside watching. Cameras were everywhere, though, and paranoia and a racing heartbeat made her use her foot to slide it farther into the room's shadows and under the bed.

Returning to her one spot of comfort, feeble as it was, she lay down and listened to the sounds around her. A guard paced the second floor where her cell was located. Prisoners on the south wall murmured through the bars to each other. The HVAC system keeping the temperature at a generous seventy-five degrees year round hummed in the background.

The guard told the talkers to shut up, but once he was gone, they continued their conversation for another few minutes.

After half an hour, the rustles and creaks of those settling in for the night ceased. A few folks snored. Others flicked on contraband lights and read or did puzzles.

Vivi slid the book from its hiding place and tucked it into bed with her. A tiny packet fell from the pages.

Inside were three gummy bears and a note. The scent of lime hit her nostrils and the memory of a man filled her head. She nearly dropped the packet and the slim edition, closing her eyes against the onslaught. His irises, as green as mountain forests, deepening with anger—or desire—to the color of the sea on a stormy day...

No. It wasn't possible. Lt. Commander Ian Kincaid didn't work for Beatrice. He was a SEAL who'd completed dozens of missions in counterterrorism and special reconnaissance.

It couldn't be him.

While her mind spun with the scenarios this presented, she considered the facts. Even if Beatrice had recruited him for this precise mission, he would have refused. The only time he'd ever failed since Vivi had been his assigned therapist was because of her. That night in Berlin.

Thing was, he didn't even know it.

He thought she was dead. The rest of the world believed she'd died that night, as well. That a traitor had gotten what she deserved.

Somedays Vivi felt like they were right. Stuck in this place, she might as well be dead and buried.

With trembling fingers and racing pulse, she shifted, setting the candy aside and angling the note so one of the faded bars of light illuminated the block text written on it.

2300 hours.

Eat all three.

No less.

Then eat this note.

She didn't recognize the handwriting, but the MO was Ian's.

When you have eliminated the impossible, whatever remains, however improbable, must be the truth.

Ian. To see him again. To try and explain...

She swallowed the ball of pain working its way up from her chest and eyed the candy again. What was in the cute little bears? Was she willing to risk her life to do as instructed?

What is freedom worth to you?

How many times had she asked her patients that? Most of the elite and highly-trained operatives never hesitated with their answer—*everything.*

People like Ian put it all on the line for their country, again and again and again. The pain they endured, not only physically, but emotionally and mentally, never went away.

Trident, her baby, had combined the best of neuroplasticity exercises, behavioral, and hypnotherapies—a three-pronged approach—to help her patients. Who was helping them now?

The final problem—could she be like those men and women who'd confessed their deepest secrets to her? Who struggled every day with the things they'd witnessed, only to get up and do it again to protect their loved ones? To keep their country safe? To be the silent heroes nobody knew or talked about?

Vivi fingered one of the bears, the lime scent once more reminding her of her own failed mission. Her cardinal rule had always been not to fall in love with a patient. Especially not a SEAL. She'd succeeded admirably until Ian. He'd been her most problematic—and most rewarding—case. He'd always had gummy bears with him. Always preferred the green ones.

Lt. Commander Kincaid didn't know she was still alive. He'd been instructed to administer a cocktail of drugs in order to remove her from Lawrence's compound. The U.S. government couldn't let her fall into enemy hands—she knew too much. Their greatest asset for keeping those in the field active and viable had become their most dangerous weapon. One that could be turned on them. Wanted dead or alive. If he couldn't retrieve her, he was ordered to terminate her.

The paradox for her came when the interrogators told her what they'd done, letting him believe he'd killed her, but she could remedy that by telling them what had happened between her and Lawrence. She couldn't remember, and therefore hadn't been able to take that offer. Pointless, anyway. She knew they'd never let her talk to Ian. To anyone.

If he now realized she was alive...

Her quiet laugh was brittle. Knowing him, he'd be happy to kill her all over again. For real, this time.

Find the answer, she heard her father say. *Every puzzle has one.*

She eyed the cute bear. "Are you poison or freedom?"

The clock was ticking. Whatever drugs were in these needed time to work before her midnight rescue.

The only way out of here is in a body bag, she'd told Beatrice. The woman, her equal in so many ways, hadn't disagreed.

"I'll be damned," she whispered to the tiny bears, shaking her head. "She's using the same trick."

Climbing from the mattress, candies in hand, she peeked out through the bars at the main clock on the wall at the far end of the corridor. Three minutes to eleven. 2300 hours was almost upon her.

"What's it going to be?" she asked herself. *Die in here, or out there?*

What is freedom worth?

Beatrice wanted fifteen minutes—to answer questions? Divulge classified information? Give her background intel on one of her employees?

Vivi considered the fact that Beatrice might be working for NSA again, or somebody who wanted answers about Jim Lawrence. Had Command & Control sucked her back in?

She discarded the idea as soon as it hit. Beatrice had been burned by the same folks who'd tossed Vivi in here. She wouldn't aid them now, although why would she care about Lawrence?

Two minutes.

Vivi glanced at the book. What would Sherlock do?

Her brilliant, but crazy, father had introduced her to the character. Asked her that a million times when Vivi was young and went to her father for help, whether it had been with homework or how to make friends.

Her mind wasn't as clear and sharp as it had been before everything went down. Hard to keep it honed and functioning well in here.

Sherlock had taken on his arch nemesis. Had lost, only to rise like the phoenix from the ashes, thanks to his creator, and make a comeback.

Everyone thought he was dead. That he'd went over that waterfall.

Everyone thought she was dead. Was it time to rise and show the world she wasn't?

Carefully, she tiptoed to her mind palace where the

memories were locked away of that night. Of Jim Lawrence.

Of Ian Kincaid.

One minute.

What if she came forward and exposed what she knew to the world? Would placing her trust in Beatrice, in Ian, be her undoing? Or would it be true freedom? To rid herself of the very thing that kept her imprisoned?

Backing away from the door of those memories, she blew out a tight, nervous breath. Slowly, she returned to the cot and lay down.

This was it. There wouldn't be another offer, another invitation. She would rot here or be assassinated. One way or the other she and everything inside her head would be extinguished.

She couldn't let that happen. Like the heroes whose secrets she had kept, she had to close off the fear and compartmentalize the what-ifs. She had a decision to make, and the former courage she'd always relied on to dig up.

Placing the first gummy bear against her lips, she closed her eyes and prayed that Ian wasn't the man sent to rescue her. Prayed that when he found out she was alive, that he didn't hate her for it.

Because in the end, her life had cost him dearly. To believe she was a traitor, had betrayed their country—and him. No amount of compartmentalizing or therapy would ever make that right.

Viv took a deep breath and ate the first gummy bear.

THREE

Not her. Couldn't be. Dr. Genevieve "Vivi" Montgomery was dead.

The weak overhead light made her face wan. Without makeup, she looked younger, tired.

Dead.

"Get her shoulders." Mick Ranger's tone had a bite to it, snapping Ian out of his shock. "I'll get her feet."

The woman on the cot in this bare bones cell had already been declared dead. He and Ranger were pretending to be from the coroner's office. Why had no one warned him that he'd be picking up a ghost?

I will kill you, Beatrice.

But not yet. This was his mission. His questions and the goddamn answers he wanted would have to wait.

Ignoring Vivi's pale skin and unmoving chest, he did as instructed. Ranger had gone over the details and the protocols with him *ad nauseam,* as if this were his first op.

Now, Ian knew why—the bastard had known their target tonight was going to shake him to his core.

Follow orders. Don't get distracted. How many times had Ranger drilled that into his head?

Like he was some newbie, a fresh recruit.

He was in a way. He was new to Shadow Force, but not to covert affairs.

Fuckin' A. You couldn't die twice. Maybe this was her doppelgänger. Some long lost twin she hadn't known about.

Or hadn't bothered to tell him about.

Neither of them had any family to speak of. Her parents were both dead; he'd never known his. But they'd promised each other they would create their own. That they would...

Ranger cleared his throat.

Under the watchful eyes of the guard posted at the open iron door, Ian grabbed her too-thin shoulders and Ranger said, "One, two, three." They team-lifted her onto the gurney with the black bag already unzipped and waiting.

I killed her.

The bag had a side zipper, rather than on top. The teeth snagged on her shirt sleeve and he tugged at it. Frustration gnawed at him under his skin when it refused to budge. He jerked so hard, the damn thing broke.

His team leader gave him an evil glare then shot a furtive glance at the book that had fallen to the floor. Beside it was a plastic wrapper.

Ian retrieved both, his gloved fingers slipping the items

into an evidence bag. He set the bag on top of the doctor's stomach.

Memories rushed back. The way she'd forced him to face his emotions after the hardest missions. How she'd refused his advances once it became clear he was desperately in love with her. She'd been the ultimate challenge—his greatest mountain to climb. Session by session, he'd worked on her as much as she had on him.

In his mind, he heard her laughter when he tickled her, once more saw her bare skin beckoning to him. The way she'd moaned his name, begged him to bring her to climax again and again, made his chest tight.

She'd been there for him each and every time he'd returned from a mission. She'd listened to all of his doubts and fears, and never once judged him. She'd lifted the burden of his childhood secrets, sharing that weight, and helping him get over a bad case of PTSD.

In the dark hours, after he'd accidentally killed her, he'd cried. Raged against himself. Nearly ended it all because of what he'd done.

"Leave it." Ranger was glaring at him again. Ian hadn't even realized he was still trying to close up the zipper. The guard held out a clipboard and Ranger took it, signing off on the form. "The autopsy report will be emailed to those listed within seventy-two hours," he told the man, deadpan. As if he did this every day. "Hope the rest of your night is quiet."

The guard groused as he accepted the clipboard. The short, fat man stood in the opening, the room too small for all three of them, plus the gurney. "Me, too. Fucking prisoners."

Ian clamped his jaw. Poor guy, having to attend to a dead woman's body instead of dozing off in front of the security cameras behind locked doors. Rough life.

Since the zipper was broken, he left the top of the bag's material draped over her. Ranger gripped the other end of the gurney and they headed out. As they bumped over the cell's threshold, one of her hands slid out from under the fabric.

Shit, even as a corpse, she just wouldn't cooperate. He tucked it back next to her side.

The wheels made a soft swishing noise on the worn tiles. Other prisoners watched with vacant eyes as they whisked her away.

Ian was sweating by the time they made it through the multiple lockdown areas and out into the night. He didn't miss Ranger taking a deep, steadying breath himself. Rumor around SFI had it that the guy had broken out of at least three, possibly up to eight various international prisons. Places so bad this one looked like an amusement park.

Together they loaded their cargo into the rear of the van disguised to look like the coroner's vehicle. 'Hell On Wheels' someone had named the transport, and they all called her Hell. Still feeling the eyes of the guards on them and avoiding looking directly at the security cameras dotting the stations and fences, they climbed into the front and Ranger wheeled them out.

They had to cross several checkpoints, all of which went smoothly until the very last. The guard inside the hut not big enough to turn around in, read over their paperwork with a slow, deliberate eye. He asked for their IDs, even though he'd already seen them when they'd entered and had called a number to verify they were legit.

Ian thought he might pull his weapon, hidden in the door and shoot the guy, especially when the man insisted on seeing the deceased.

"I'm about forty-eight hours short on sleep," he growled at the guard. "What the fuck you want to see a dead body for? That get you off, or something?"

Ranger shot him another quelling glare. "It's no problem," he ground out, before he exited the cab and walked the guard to the rear. He opened the double doors. "See? Only our corpse."

Ian peeled his weapon from its hidden compartment when the asshole climbed in and shone his flashlight all around, ending with checking out Vivi by lifting the top of the bag and spotlighting her slack face.

The safety might have *accidentally* flicked off his gun. He counted to ten, waiting, ready.

The doors slammed shut. Ranger returned to the driver's seat. The guard handed him their IDs and the paperwork through his open window.

Ian slipped the gun down on the side of his seat, out of view.

"Y'all have a good night now," the man said, tapping the side of the van twice and giving Ian the finger.

Ranger accelerated and Ian tucked the gun away. In silence, they drove, and as soon as they cleared the grounds, Ian shifted into gear.

The passenger door wasn't the only one with a secret compartment. Flinging the top of the body bag off Vivi's face, he slid the evidence bag into a container that would be incinerated once they were at HQ. A flip of a switch and he had enough light to see by. Inside his coveralls, he located the vial of adrenaline and removed a syringe from the medical kit Dr. Jaxon Sloan had sent along. SFI's on-staff doctor should have been delivering the injection, but Beatrice had insisted Ian do the honors.

Now he understood why.

"You fucking should have told me," he yelled at Ranger.

"Told you what?"

Ian grumbled to himself, calling Ranger every name in the book as he prepped Vivi's arm and the syringe. "I will kill each and every one of you when this is over. Slowly. With great satisfaction at the amount of pain I will inflict."

Ranger laughed. Fucking *laughed*. "What the fuck is wrong with you? The Queen B told you there were missions that sucked and none are glorious. You joined our team, and this is the type of shit we do."

He didn't know Ian's connection to the woman on the gurney? Thought he was upset over a prison break?

Maybe he wouldn't kill him. Did Beatrice know, or was this some weird karmic Murphy's Law thing coming around to haunt him?

He took a breath, steadying his hands before he injected the adrenaline. "Never mind."

"To be honest," Ranger said, "this is a rare one. Most of our missions involve rescues, but this is the first one I've done where the target was pretending to be dead."

Ian watched as the last of the liquid went into Vivi's vein. Jaxon had told him it would take approximately five to ten seconds for her to revive. He tossed the used needle into the sharps container, at the same time counting off the seconds on his watch.

Five, four...

"Uh oh." The van began to decelerate and Ranger glanced in the rearview at him. "We've got trouble. Get back up here."

Two, one...

Vivi gasped, her body jackknifing straight up. Ian caught her by the shoulders. "What the fuck?" he asked Ranger. "What kind of trouble?"

At that moment, a revolving blue light cut through the windshield and raked over them. Vivi's eyes were clouded and she continued to gasp for air. Confusion knit her brows and she gripped Ian's arms.

"Can't outrun 'em." The van slid to the side of the road, kicking up gravel. Ranger glanced over his shoulder and ordered, "Get her back in the body bag and get your ass up here. *Now.*"

Like that was gonna happen. Ian slammed her down on the gurney. "Vivi, listen to me. You have to play dead. Don't move. Don't breathe. No matter what happens."

A hint of recognition crossed her face, and on its heels, fear. "Ian?"

Her voice was raspy, but even so, he found his own breath stick in his chest. God, he'd missed her. Her voice, her smile. Regardless of what was happening, all he wanted to do was grab her and squeeze. Prove to himself she was really alive.

Her breathing evened out and her eyes cleared. His relief at that fact didn't take away the anger boiling under his skin over the subterfuge, but now wasn't the time to dive into either that or his fucked up feelings about her.

He shut down his emotions, like the good soldier he was. "Play dead," he commanded, and then flipped the material back over her face. "Or you really will be."

FOUR

Everything came rushing back at once. Waking in a body bag was a nightmare. Feeling like she was in space hovering over herself had seemed like a dream.

But when she'd heard a set of men's voices a few feet away, she'd realized it was neither a dream, nor her worst nightmare.

Beatrice had come through. Vivi was free. Sure, she was in the rear of what she assumed was a coroner's van, and something was wrong, but she could breathe again.

Play dead. Ian's voice rang in her ears, even as she trembled from the adrenaline coursing through it. Her brain wasn't fully online, and her CIA training was far in the past, yet some deep-seated survival instinct kicked in when the door squeaked open.

"A single corpse," she heard one of them say. Not Ian; the driver. "The paperwork is all here, Officer."

The beam of a flashlight teased the edges of the bag.

She wondered why Ian hadn't closed it—that was sure to give them away, wasn't it?

Holding her breath, she steeled her body to keep it from trembling. She was out of that horrible place, and she would *not* go back, no matter what. She'd take a stand here rather than ending up inside a prison again.

The owner of the flashlight climbed in, causing the back end to dip slightly. Forcing herself into her mind palace, she entered her favorite room, full of peace and comfort and...

She nearly jumped when the man patted her foot.

Bastard. He felt his way up her calf, making sure the lump under the fabric was human and not hiding drugs or other contraband.

Don't breathe, don't breathe.

The hand stopped at her hip. "Why's the zipper open?"

"Cheap-ass thing broke," Ian drawled, his voice close to her head as if he were leaning over her from between the front seats.

All she needed was for the officer to—

He flipped the suffocating fabric off her face and cool air tickled her cheeks. As if she could read his mind, she heard Ian say *play dead, or you really will be.*

Barreling down into herself, she went back to her mental Zen room. She watched her birds fly around the space and twitter at her.

And then the scene shifted. She was suddenly across from the man who'd just shoved adrenaline into her heart and ordered her to act like a corpse. *Sure, no problem.*

He stared at her across the coffee table between them.

He was cocky and impatient, hating the fact he was required after every mission to come see her. Rules and regulations weren't his style, and she'd made it her own personal mission to change his perspective on therapy.

She smiled at him and slowly, giving into her charm, he returned it.

Her memories kicked in and she was in Vegas with him, in bed. He was laughing and kissing her and...

The officer grunted. "Pretty one. Hell, she doesn't even look dead."

She sensed him bending close, as if checking for the warmth of her breath. *Don't move.*

A tense second passed. Another. She had the feeling she wasn't the only one holding their breath. Ian and his partner had to be shitting bricks.

If they all escaped this, they were going to be damn lucky.

The officer reeked of onions, but finally he seemed satisfied. Good thing, too, since Vivi was out of air, lungs burning.

The van rocked as the officer jumped down. "Have a good night now," he said, and the squawk of his radio echoed around them, a call coming in.

The door closed; silence filled her ears. Another slammed—the driver getting back in. Slowly, he pulled out from the side of the road and they accelerated.

Gripping the edges of the gurney, Vivi sat up and drew in the deepest breath she'd ever taken. Oxygen had never felt so good.

The two men were still silent, but she couldn't help it. She laughed. The rush of what had just happened, fueled by the adrenaline in her veins, filled her with giddiness. *I'm alive.*

Free.

"What the actual fuck?"

She looked around to see Ian glaring at her from the passenger seat. He looked good, although still haunted by his past. Their past.

She had a lot of explaining to do. She only hoped he would listen. And maybe someday, he might forgive her.

Fat chance, that. Swinging her legs to the side, she steadied herself. Was it too much to hope that they could start over?

She knew the answer. While she'd always been an optimist, she wasn't a fool. He would never forgive, nor forget, her betrayal.

A chill swept over her and she visibly shivered. After-effects of the drugs, she told herself. It had nothing to do with Ian seeking revenge.

"You did good back there," the driver called. "My name's Mick."

"I know who you are, Lieutenant Ranger."

"My reputation precedes me." He seemed proud of that. "Afraid I'm not a lieutenant anymore, ma'am. Not even a frogman these days." He took a turn and nothing but the dark night and empty highway could be seen through the windshield. "I believe you already know my partner."

"You *did* know. Fucking bastard." Ian sounded livid.

"Beatrice may have mentioned it."

Ian punched the dash. "That important detail would've been nice to share."

"Would you have come?" Ranger asked.

Ian didn't answer. An answer in itself.

There were consequences to every action, and many of hers had been less than ideal. Especially when it came to the man with the dark hair and the pine green eyes now watching her every move. The consequence of falling in love with him had cost her much—nearly her life—but he'd paid a price no one should have to—believing someone they loved was dead at his own hands.

Scrounging around, she found a thin gray blanket and wrapped it around herself. Her teeth chattered and she felt woozy, the night's events slamming into her with the fierceness that would take days to sleep off.

Or maybe, it was the result of the daggers he was shooting at her.

She gave him a wan smile. "Hello, husband."

FIVE

T*he next morning*
SFI headquarters

IAN BURST through Beatrice's door. "What the actual fu—"

"Stop!" she yelled over him, pen rising into the air. She pointed toward the corner as the door hit the wall.

Her daughter, Sloane, was wide-eyed, fear causing her to scoot back on her playmat where she was sitting at her own miniature desk, mimicking her mother. Jeez, he was a douche.

Connor rushed in on Ian's heels, placing himself between him and Beatrice. "He got past me while I was on a call with Emit." The man looked far younger than his years but his face was red with fury. He was Beatrice's attack dog, as well as her assistant. "Stand down, Kincaid, or I'll escort you to the exit."

Ian calculated the odds that he could take the guy, but not in front of the kid. "Sorry," he said to Beatrice. "I didn't know she was in here."

"Obviously." Beatrice smiled at Sloane. "It's okay, sweetie. Why don't you go downstairs with Uncle Connor and get some ice cream?"

"Can I?" She jumped up, grabbing her favorite stuffed dog, and ran to Connor, who lifted her. "Can Uncle Idol come too?"

His own anger fading, Ian patted her head. She tended to call all of them by their codenames. "Maybe later, okay, stinkbug?"

"I don't stink!" In the three weeks since he'd arrived, it had become a running joke between them. "*You* stink!"

Connor glanced at Beatrice and she nodded, letting him know she would handle Ian. The man then narrowed his eyes at him over Sloane's head in a silent threat as he carried the girl out and shut the door.

"Sit down," Beatrice said in a no-nonsense tone. "And don't ever raise your voice to me again."

Ian seethed and refused the chair she pointed at. "You knew she was alive and you kept it from me. Are you a fucking sadist?"

She tipped back in her chair and stared at him with speculation. "I only discovered this a few days ago and I needed to see her, talk to her, before I did anything."

She didn't pull punches. Neither did he. "Bullshit. You were testing me to see how I did under pressure."

"Every mission has surprises. You know that. You also know you need to expect to be blindsided at times."

"You're a cold-hearted bitch."

"Careful, Mr. Kincaid, or I'll escort you out of SFI myself." They glared at each other. "The men and women who work for me are my highest priority, outside of Cal and Sloane. You came to me asking for a job; I gave you one. Part of the reason Genevieve was behind bars is due to you, so I deemed it wise to have you involved in her rescue. You and I both know she is no traitor, and I need you to help me figure out how to prove it."

Finally, he sat, but couldn't relax, staying on the edge of the seat. "The problem is, I *don't* know that."

"It's my turn to call bullshit. She may not have been in the field, but that woman took all of your mental dreck, as well as that of hundreds more, and bottled it up inside her. Why? Certainly not for glory or fame. No one will ever know the extent that she has gone to in order to keep you and her other patients functioning at their highest potential. While I may be a *cold-hearted bitch*, as you so eloquently put it, she has compassion in spades. She's a hero, in my book. If you disagree with what I've done, don't let the door hit you in the ass on the way out."

She dropped her gaze to the folder in front of her and began making a note.

Ian stood, debating his choices. Stay and confront his wife, or leave and... Do what? Hit the unemployment line and hope to fill a slot somewhere? Wonder for the rest of his life if Vivi was guilty or not? He had no family he could stay with. His best friends were still in the Navy.

With the exception of the woman recovering on the

third floor, and the one now ignoring him, he had no one and nothing.

"I'm sorry for calling you a bitch," he said, and he was. "My temper gets the best of me at times."

"I've noticed." She still didn't look at him. "We all have our triggers—Sloane and Cal are mine. She's yours." Finishing her note, she glanced up. "You're not the first, nor will you be the last man to storm in here and yell at me, by the way. Unlike Dr. Montgomery, I tend to get under people's skin. Part of making sure everybody here is always safe is guaranteeing no one fails on a mission. No one. Not you, not Cal, not any of the others. I have to know without a doubt that you can and will complete every mission I give you. Unexpected things will happen and you have to be able to compensate for them in order to protect your teammates and this organization. Do you understand?"

What else was there to say? It pained him, but he nodded. "Understood. Still have a spot for me in this organization?"

She shooed him off. "You passed your test. Your probationary period is over. Now, go downstairs and have ice cream with my daughter. Ever scare her again and you will disappear. They will never find your body."

"Roger that." He smiled to himself as he left her office.

THREE DAYS *later*

Food, rest, recovery. The classic three items needed after you've been dead and revived.

But Vivi couldn't sleep, roaming the halls of Shadow Force International's headquarters. Day and night, men and women came and went. Her room was on the third floor, and she often met others like herself who slept fitfully. All were polite but none seemed interested in who she was or why she was there.

She liked it that way. The cafeteria in the basement was small but was constantly stocked with delicious items. Either that, or she had consumed so much prison food anything tasted good at this point. She had gorged herself three times, her stomach unable to handle the richness after the crap she'd been eating and rejecting it. She hated vomiting; but it was worth it to consume anything and everything she could, anytime she wanted it. Eventually, her stomach would accept what she was putting down her throat. She'd lost a good ten pounds behind those iron bars, and she planned to put every one of them back on, plus a few more.

Recovering physically was one thing. She wasn't sure if she would ever recover mentally or emotionally. Seeing Ian had made her both happy and sad. Beatrice had ordered him to leave Vivi alone until she was ready to talk. She was glad he'd moved on with his life, but the looks he'd given her the couple times she'd glimpsed him in the halls or cafeteria had shredded her heart.

Every nerve in her body felt hypersensitive, her defenses always on high alert. Logically, she knew this place was a fortress, but would she ever believe she was truly safe? Could she ever take her experience and turn it into something good, like Beatrice had?

Calling her by that name still felt odd, but she was

definitely a different person than the former Bianca Marx that Vivi had known during her time with Command & Control. Seemed like a lifetime ago. Maybe it was.

Before Berlin. After Berlin. So much had changed the moment she had walked in to Lawrence's compound.

Even with Beatrice's order, Vivi suspected Ian was avoiding her. He'd never even looked back when he deposited her in the medical ward and Jaxon Sloan had taken over.

The physician had given her sleeping pills, but the thought of being that out of it scared her. She'd never liked feeling out of control, even when asleep. She hated dreaming, although she knew it was a door to the subconscious. Never letting on about her dislike to her patients, she'd probed theirs with strategic efficiency.

Time would heal her physical body, rebalance her stomach, and maybe even allow her to sink into a deep sleeping state at some point. Knowing Ian was around eased her stress and fear. He'd always made her feel safe, and though he didn't want anything to do with her at the moment, she secretly sought him out. Watched him from the shadows, listened to his voice as he spoke to his friends and coworkers in the halls and cafeteria. She made sure he never saw her, but like a touchstone, his simple presence calmed her anxiety.

Three days. How much longer could she stay here? She hated being in anyone's debt, but her mind palace was not cooperating. No matter how she tried to unlock a certain door, she couldn't.

Standing outside of Beatrice's office, she took a steadying breath. *Time to face the music.*

Bursting in, she huffed out what she needed to say. "I don't remember."

Beatrice had on a starched white shirt, just like Vivi remembered her always wearing. Her crystal blue eyes looked startled behind thick framed glasses, and her hair was carefully contained in a neat bun.

The dog next to the desk, a black lab named Maggie, lifted her head. Her pink studded collar twinkled under the lights.

A man was in a chair across from her, and sized Vivi up with a bored glance. He appeared older than most at SFI, with hard eyes and a scruffy beard, and he grabbed a tablet from the top of the massive desk as if his meeting with Beatrice was over, thanks to her. He slid it into a leather carrier attached to his chest and snatched up a set of crutches from the floor. "I managed to unfreeze the majority of your assets," he said to Vivi as he struggled to his feet. "The rest will take more time." He checked the expensive sports watch on his left wrist once he'd settled his armpits on the crutches. "Need another sixteen hours, give or take."

Shaky on the crutches, but seemingly determined, he passed her. "What's your favorite color?" he asked as he did.

"What?"

He met her eyes. "Simple question, Doc. What's your favorite color?"

"Green," she answered, sending Beatrice a questioning look.

He nodded and shut the door behind him.

Beatrice sat back and motioned her into the chair.

"That's Rory. Former CIA assassin. Don't know if you ever met him in your time counseling spies."

Vivi shook her head, glad she hadn't.

"He was crippled in an attack trying to save me," Beatrice went on. "He's getting the use of his legs back after being paralyzed for a long time. He believed he was done for, sidelined, and he probably would've put a gun to his head if I hadn't insisted he take over my cyber unit. I believe his paralysis is more mental than physical."

The dog came to its feet and sniffed Vivi's hand. She'd seen it occasionally with Cal, and heard stories about the therapy canines SFI now trained and had available to those who needed them.

Beatrice rocked back and forth and fiddled with a Mont Blanc pen. "What don't you remember?"

Vivi patted the dog's head before she dropped into the vacated chair, and worried her fingers in her lap. Ironic that the only thing Beatrice and everyone else wanted from her was buried in her mind. "Your fifteen minutes with me is pointless. I know what you want and I can't give you the information because I ..." The void rushed up, a tsunami. She could remember up to a certain point, then...nothing. Until she woke in a helicopter, cuffed and labeled a traitor. The information she wanted desperately to recall was trapped behind a thick, solid, and neatly impenetrable steel door.

Even now when she teased at the lock of the blockade, her body flinched as if she'd been shocked. She unclasped her hands and grabbed the chair's arm rests, digging her nails into the wood. Her voice came out a rasp. "I don't remember what happened that night."

A child's voice came from behind her. "Mommy?"

Vivi turned in the seat and sucked in a breath. A mini version of Beatrice strolled slowly toward her mother on chubby toddler legs, keeping her big blue eyes pinned on Vivi.

She hadn't even noticed how large the office was, or the playmat taking up an entire corner underneath a window. Toys were everywhere, including a dollhouse, kitchenette, and a trunk of dress-up clothes.

The single thing on the mat not a toy moved lazily. Ian kicked out his long legs, crossing them at the ankles. He and the girl had been playing with an assortment of dinosaurs, and he glanced away as Vivi met his eyes.

Children. They'd talked about them, wanted them. After he completed his final assignment. After she'd turned in her resignation. After...

Vivi pivoted back to look at Beatrice and the pint-sized girl. "Dr. Montgomery." Beatrice lifted the child and tucked her onto her lap. "I'd like you to meet my daughter, Sloane."

Sloane like the doctor? Interesting.

"Yes," Beatrice added, sensing her question. "After Jaxon. He means a great deal to me."

Vivi stood, attention torn between the tiny double and the man glaring at her from a fortress of colorful play things. "Nice to meet you." To Beatrice, she said, "Excuse my interruption. I didn't realize... You're busy. I'll make an appointment with your assistant and come back later."

"Let's talk now." Beatrice rose, setting Sloane on her hip. "It's time for her nap."

"No nap," the girl exclaimed. "Not tired." At the same

time, she dropped her head to her mother's shoulder and rubbed her eyes.

"I can take her." Ian joined them. "I'll even read to you for a few minutes," he said, reaching out his arms.

Beatrice gave a small shake of her head. "I have a better idea. How about we take a ride? Uncle Ian will read to you later, okay?"

"Yes!" The girl did an adorable tiny fist pump. Maggie barked. "Uncle Idol come, too?"

Idol? Vivi scrutinized him. Rock Star Security provided bodyguards and a solid, law-abiding front for Shadow Force International, the unit that provided private intelligence, security, and paramilitary missions for those who had nowhere else to turn. They all used rock star code names—was that his?

Ian glanced at the door—ready to escape? "I have work, stinkbug."

"We could use a driver." Beatrice winked at him over Sloane's head. "And maybe a drive will put you-know-who to sleep."

Sloane pointed a tiny finger at her mother's face. "No sleep."

Ian's lips firmed—he didn't like the idea, and Vivi had one guess as to why—her. He kept his attention on the child and his boss. "I'll bring the car around."

Without a backward glance, he left them. Beatrice retrieved a bag from her bottom drawer, never putting her daughter down. "I don't care about that information. Don't stress over it. You've been through an ordeal, and it's not surprising you're repressing the very thing that caused it. You'll remember in time."

Sweat broke out around Vivi's hairline. The thought of leaving the building, this fortress, made her legs tremble. She forced courage into them. "Then what is this? What do you want to ask me?"

Ian hadn't fully shut the door as he'd left and now another man entered. Callan Reece. He pulled up short when he saw Vivi. Maggie rushed to his side and he greeted the dog, saying to Vivi, "Good to see you out and about. How are you adjusting, Dr. Montgomery?"

It seemed weird being referred to her by her professional label. "Vivi, please. I'm doing as well as can be expected, I suppose."

Sloane reached for him and he lifted her from her mother's hold. "Some of us attend peer support group meetings down the block once a week, or whenever we're in town. You're welcome to join us."

Caught off guard, she wondered what she, a highly trained psychologist, could gain from such a group. Probably a hell of a lot. "Thank you. When I feel more"— *safe* —"up to it, I'd love to attend."

"We're going to check on the new site," Beatrice told him. "Care to ride along?"

"I wish." He kissed the child's head. "I'm due at the Justice Department in an hour to speak to—" He glanced at Vivi. "Anyway, I can't, but I wanted to see if we were still on for dinner. I don't leave for..." Another look at Vivi before he reined in what must have been classified details. "*You know*, until 0800 hours."

Beatrice kissed him. "Of course."

He raspberried Sloane's cheek, making her giggle before he put her down. "See you tonight."

They said their goodbyes, Maggie leaving with Cal. Beatrice gathered her phone and purse before taking the child's hand. "Shall we?"

Vivi swallowed the dryness in her mouth. "I don't think it's a good idea. I'll stay here and we can speak later."

"You're safe. You need to get out and get some fresh air. I want to show you my latest project. I'm hoping you'll play a role in it."

Challenge flashed in her eyes. Vivi silently cursed. This was why she didn't like owing anyone a debt—they could call it in at any moment, leaving you off-balance.

But what else did she have to do? In three days, when she wasn't puking after gorging on food, and since she couldn't get any sleep, she'd already read through half the books in the library. While her self-inflicted confinement was certainly better than a prison cell, she was growing bored. She'd even agreed to a game of Chinese checkers with a woman in the cafeteria earlier. Sabrina, the lab supervisor. Flamboyant red hair and a sapphire blue jumpsuit, she'd had a light, airy humor about her, even in the heat of their game.

Such a simple thing, yet Vivi had forgotten her problems for a few minutes while she strategized getting her green marbles across the board. It had been...freeing. No guilt or shame. No clawing memories or fear of the future. Sabrina had made her promise a rematch after Vivi had won, and she found she was looking forward to it. She followed Beatrice into the hall. "How long will we be gone?"

"You have something pressing to get back to?" Beatrice pressed the down button.

Smartass. "Am I dressed appropriately?"

The woman looked over her jeans and T-shirt. "You'll fit right in."

Downstairs, a slick, black, all-terrain vehicle pulled up at the rear exit. Tinted windows, and Vivi suspected bulletproof reinforced steel, surrounded them as they left and merged into traffic.

Vivi didn't feel comfortable discussing her earlier concerns with the child and Ian in hearing range, so she asked questions, listening as Beatrice gave her the history of SFI, and then explained the significance of the new compound.

The girl did not fall asleep, fighting it with the willpower of a pit bull. Vivi had never seen herself as a mother until Ian had come along. Since her incarceration, that dream had died along with everything else. Now, she found herself entertained by the child. Sloane had her mother's spunk, and Vivi found she rather liked her.

Twenty minutes later, they arrived at a gated entrance. Once through that, a sprawling acreage spread out around them, complete with buildings, a central parking area, and what appeared to be a lake in the distance. Nestled at the foot of a mountain range, the smell of evergreen trees invaded the car and Vivi breathed deeply.

Earth moving equipment and contractors crisscrossed the grounds, shouts and the engine sounds of revving motors filling the air. Ian had to navigate around building supplies and playground equipment yet to be installed.

"What is this place?" Vivi asked.

A warm smile tweaked the corners of Beatrice's mouth. "Home," she said.

SIX

Beatrice gave Vivi a tour under Ian's watchful eyes. Men and women in overalls were everywhere, a few he recognized from his regular visits here with Beatrice. While on his probationary period, he'd been her designated driver. The sound of hammers, saws, and shouted instructions filled the air, drowning out the birds in the woods as well as the lapping waves of the lake.

He tried not to stare at his wife, not to demand the answers he needed.

What I need is her.

He tried to scrub that thought from his brain, rubbing his knuckles over his short, terse hair. He did *not* need her, no matter what his heart kept demanding.

"The place was originally owned by an inventor in the seventies who sold multiple patents to the U.S. government," Beatrice was telling Vivi as they walked slightly ahead of him. She pointed to a brick building on the right. "That housed the original offices. We're remodeling them for professional services—medical, mental health, legal—for our employees."

Ian didn't miss the way Vivi's attention flicked to Beatrice at the mention of mental health. He could tell her brain instantly realized one of the reasons why she'd been rescued. It was news to him, too.

This was a recruitment. "You have that many employees?" Vivi crossed her arms at Beatrice's nod. "And who pays for those services?"

"We provide them free of charge. The combination of Rock Star Security and Shadow Force International is profitable, but many of our personnel are dealing with a host of issues when they come to us. They often need intervention before they are field ready." Ignoring Vivi's scrutiny, Beatrice continued on. Behind the older building loomed a three-story modern addition. Sunlight glinted off the windows. Beatrice pointed to it. "That section is being turned into living quarters. We have approximately fifty-six onsite employees who need housing. We have learned that they are happier and healthier if they don't have to worry about finding a place to live or scrounging for meals."

Vivi's tone was light. Even so, her words had an edge to them. "It appears you've formed your own cult."

Beatrice laughed it off. She shifted to peer left, drawing Vivi's attention to the landscape in the distance. As they continued to steer clear of the construction, a shaft of soft sunlight cut through the trees and sparkled in his wife's hair.

The memory of how soft it was, how it smelled like peaches from her shampoo, how it felt when his fingers were tangled in it, made his gut tight. Even after what she'd done, he still wanted her.

Beatrice pointed across the water. "The mountain, the caves, this lake—they're all good for search and rescue training. We've already installed a gun range and we'll be off the grid, using solar and wind energy. I've planned out a community garden, too."

Vivi shook her head and snorted. "I've got to admit, it's impressive."

Beatrice gently rocked Sloane, whose lids kept fluttering closed. "We're a family, and this place will allow us to house, feed, and train with fewer restrictions."

"You'll live here?"

Beatrice nodded. "Our family is at SFI round the clock, anyway. We rarely make it home, even to sleep."

"No sleep," Sloane murmured, even as she was losing the battle with it. "Please, Mommy. No bad dreams."

Ian's gut cramped again. He liked the kid; in the past few months, she'd filled the emptiness in his chest when he'd believed he'd never have children. He wasn't cut out for fatherhood now, though. Not with his messed up head and a wife who was supposed to be a traitor. A *dead* traitor.

In their short time together, they'd discussed having a family. At first, Vivi had claimed she didn't want any. When he pressed her as to why, she told him she feared her father's mental issues might be hereditary. Sensing he might never have a son or daughter now, Ian's heart gave a pang.

Beatrice kissed the girl's head. "Sloane is experiencing nightmares. We're not sure why."

"I'm sorry to hear that." Vivi reached over and patted the girl on the back. "I don't like them either. Unfortunately, they're a part of life. We all have them."

Sloane made a fist and shook it in the air. "No sleep. No bad dreams."

Ian smiled to himself. If he ever did have a child, he hoped they would have as much pluck as she did.

Beatrice stared at the doctor over Sloane. "Any thoughts? She can't go without sleep. In spite of that, these nightmares are out of hand. We need help."

Vivi faced Beatrice head on, and Ian almost took a step back. The fierceness in her face took him by surprise. "You. Can't. Be. Serious."

Ian frowned. Was this the real reason Beatrice had broken her out of prison? He thought she was recruiting Vivi for all of them—the men and women of SFI. The ones who were struggling with their demons, PTSD, and nightmares, just like Sloane.

How wrong he'd been.

He'd give anything if he could take the child's bad dreams away. Even as horrible as his were, he would gladly take on hers.

"That's why you don't care about the Lawrence fiasco." Vivi's eyes narrowed, her voice a cutting accusation. "That's why you brought me here."

"I sent Ian to rescue you because you didn't deserve to be in that hellhole."

"Cut the bull—" Vivi pinched her lips together, cutting herself off as she remembered there was a child present. Ian saw her hands ball into fists, as vehement as the girl. "You're still out of luck if you think I can do anything. I'm not a child psychiatrist. You know that."

"I've had her to a specialist. He couldn't help." Sloane peeked over at Vivi, once more with her head on Beatrice's shoulder. She sucked on her thumb and Ian gave her a wink when she raised her big eyes to him. "I need someone I trust to evaluate what's going on and why. As I mentioned, I'm desperate."

Vivi pivoted and stalked away, stopped. Her shoulders were as tense as her face. Ian knew that look, that reaction. She didn't like surprises, and while she had trained herself not to react to most, this one had obviously knocked her for a loop.

He hid a grin. It took a lot to shake the good doctor, to put her in a situation where she was this torn. She owed Beatrice and they all knew it. How could she say no?

Facing the lake, her gaze snagged on the contractors installing security cameras. "How can you trust me? I don't even trust myself. My brain is as much of a mess as anyone's. You don't want me helping Sloane."

"Your brain isn't the issue," Beatrice argued. "You may have trouble accessing some of your memories, but that doesn't mean you're not still a damn good psychologist. The best."

"Bad word, Mommy," Sloane said in a sleepy voice. "A dollar in the swear jar."

Beatrice stroked her daughter's hair. "Remind me when we get back." At Vivi's questioning look, Beatrice shrugged. "Swearing is common among our group. While I don't care, I also don't want her running around using that language in public."

Ian grinned. Too late. He'd heard her swear like the best of them when she couldn't get her blocks stacked the way she wanted, or pull a shirt on her doll with ease.

Vivi rubbed the back of her neck and laughed, but the sound was dry. "I can't, Beatrice. Until I remember what happened in Berlin, I'm more of a threat than a help to all of you."

Beatrice glanced away, disappointed, but nodded. "You're welcome to stay as long as you want, regardless. You'll always have a place with us."

She carried Sloane toward the vehicle, leaving Vivi and Ian staring at each other.

Will you stay? He wanted to ask. And then he wondered why he cared.

"She did you a solid," he grumbled, not able to hold back. "We all thought you were dead, and you would've been eventually, if that woman there"—he pointed to Beatrice's back—"hadn't risked all of this to get you out. All she wants is for you to talk to her daughter and see if you can help her. Since when are you a coward?"

Once again, the doctor was taken by surprise. "You don't even know me anymore."

She was right. He'd thought he knew her, but he'd been wrong. About her and so many other things. "I'm not sure I ever did."

He turned on his heel and stalked to the car.

SEVEN

Vivi stared at the wall in her room. During their trip the previous afternoon to see the "compound"—the term she had started calling it in her mind—someone had hung a painting of a pair of lovebirds on her wall.

Invasion of privacy, sure. Some hidden meaning? Possibly. Regardless, birds made her happy, so she wasn't going to complain. *Come to me, my little bird.* She could still hear her father's voice, after all these years. If she hadn't been so upset at the compound, she would have loved trying to identify many of those in the nearby trees. She wondered who she should talk to about getting some bird books for the library.

And then, she smacked her forehead with the palm of her hand. *What am I thinking? No one here cares about birds, except me, and I won't be staying.*

So far, she was living at this headquarters rent free, which bothered her, but she didn't like being manipulated either. She was going to suck it up and see what she could do for Sloane, but she had no hope of helping. Hell, with her luck right now, she might make things worse.

Which was why she'd said no in the first place. Not because she didn't *want* to help, but, as she'd reminded Beatrice, she wasn't a child psychologist, nor was she sure of her own sanity at the moment. The past six months had tied her up—emotionally, mentally, and physically. Secrets bored into her. Gaps in her memory racked her with fear of what she'd forgotten.

And then there was Ian. Talk about nightmares.

He was so opposite of her. Tough, strong, courageous.

His comment had stung more than if he'd actually struck her. The disappointment in his eyes had nearly felled her.

Once she'd been his lifeline. Now, it seemed she was his anchor.

Vivi sighed—she'd been doing that a lot the past few days. Amends needed to be made, debts repaid. Figuring out how to do both was the problem. *Damned if I do, damned if I don't.*

The puzzle about Sloane's dreams had been consuming her. There had to be an answer, a root cause to the fear chasing the girl in her sleep.

Her brilliant, if currently unstable, mind insisted Vivi knew the reason she was fascinated by that cause. It might answer her own questions. What was she hiding from herself? Why couldn't she remember what had happened that night?

Leaving her room, her first stop was to see Rory. "Don't bother with my money," she told him. "You can bet the agency I used to work for has eyes on it. You touch it, they'll trace it—and my fake death—back to Beatrice and SFI."

The bearded man scoffed. "Nobody traces my magic." He wiggled his fingers in the air.

So cocky. "They will. Please, for all our sakes, let it be."

He sat back in his fancy, ergonomic chair and appraised her. "You're rich as Midas, and I know you earned every penny, even though you and I never crossed paths while I was a spook. Why let them have it?"

"It's the devil's money. I sold my soul for those pennies. Each and every one is tainted and I don't care that they have it. I certainly don't want it."

He made a capitulating gesture with one hand. "All right, but you are seriously underestimating my skills."

"I'm sure you're the best. I simply don't wish to bring any unwanted attention to your organization."

He nodded and his expression softened. "We've all been there, you know. Danced with the devil."

She hadn't simply danced with him. She'd been his puppet. There was no changing that. It was time to move forward and make up for it. "Since I'm broke, I could use a job. Any suggestions?"

He frowned, perplexed. "The Queen B offered you one."

"Not as a therapist." She swallowed her reservations and stiffened her resolve. "I'll do that for free. What I mean is, is there anything menial around her I can help with? Paperwork? Laundry? Cleaning?"

"A Ph.D. scrubbing toilets?"

"It's honest work."

His expression took on a look of approval. "We clean our own. Do our own laundry, too. Actual paperwork is mostly nonexistent—our internal system is paperless—but I could use someone to comb databases for me."

"Requirements?"

He grinned and showed her his collection of dirty coffee cups. "Keep me caffeinated and know how to use a computer."

"What's the pay? I need to make rent and buy a wardrobe. Nothing fancy, but some jeans that actually fit and shirts that aren't white and read Hanes on the tag."

A rough laugh. "Not up to your standards, Doc?"

"They're men's t-shirts, and while I've been known to throw one on in the past"—specifically Ian's, after a round of lovemaking—"I'd like to feel feminine again after the prison jumpsuit."

"I need you for six hours a week to start, more if you're adequate at it. That will cover your *rent*." He handed her a cup. "We mostly barter around here, our skills in exchange for a decent place to live and work. As far as the wardrobe, you'll have to talk to Beatrice about that."

Of course she would. She took the mug, found the nearest breakroom and scrubbed the stains out of it. Menial work, indeed, but it felt good to focus on something so simple. She returned with it clean and full a few minutes later. "Okay, boss, what's next?"

Two hours later, the data she'd been scanning endlessly had made her eyes bug out. She'd impressed Rory, though, finding two different links he'd been searching for to a terrorist organization on SFI's radar. "I need a break," she told him.

"I'm surprised your pointman hasn't already swooped in to get you."

"My what?"

"The person Beatrice assigned as your liaison." At her blank look, he went on. "For your first thirty days, you get an instructor, a guide, who coaches you. They walk you through how we do things here and make sure to answer your questions. We've found that assimilation back into civilian life goes smoother if there's someone you can talk to, and who checks on you regularly. None of us likes to ask for help, but you can, you know. Ian hasn't been here long himself, so he may not have all the answers. You hit me up, if need be."

"Ian?" She thought it over. "Why do you assume he's my pointman?"

"Uh, by the way he's keeping an eye on you?"

This was said with a tone suggesting she was dense. Maybe she was. She honestly hadn't been aware of him, but then he *was* a former SEAL. He knew how to move in the shadows and go unnoticed. And here, she thought she was doing that to him. "No one has informed me that I have an official guide, but thanks for the offer. Would it be possible for me to do some personal research this week?"

"Within limits, sure. As we were just discussing, it's imperative I keep our system secure."

"Of course. I certainly don't want to jeopardize that. I'll run everything past you, okay?"

He nodded, then gave her a look filled with scrutiny. "If you want to dig into your past, let me do it."

She shook her head. "My past, my research."

"I'll make sure you don't trip any wires or fall into any traps set up by Command & Control. You feel me?"

Once again, she struggled to hide her surprise. "You know about C&C?"

He gave her a cunning smile as his response.

"Okay, then. I also need to research info on child psychology and dream analysis."

"Give your eyes a rest and when you come back, I'll set you up with internet access."

"Thanks." Before she lost her nerve, she took the plunge. "I could use some intel on..."

Her throat locked up. Why couldn't she say the name? She needed to know what had gone down that night from the reports. What had been written about it afterwards. All of it would be classified.

Rory didn't miss a beat, grabbing his crutches and hauling himself up. "I've got a file you might want to look at."

"Don't go to any trouble," she started, but he sent her a silencing glance.

He retrieved a laptop from a nearby workstation and handed it to her. "Your pointman was supposed to check this out and give it to you. You can access the SFI intranet to file reports, share data, that sort of thing. No web access, but it's yours for whatever you need. You'll find copies of the classified reports in a folder marked with the date. These aren't on the intranet, only this laptop and mine."

Accepting it, she felt the tightness in her chest loosen a fraction. Another part, however, squeezed at the thought of going down this road.

He pulled a manila envelope from his desk drawer and tossed it at her. "Your new identity. It's still malleable and you can fill in the backstory in more detail any time. Enjoy."

Would she ever be able to feel normal if even her very name was different? *So much to process.*

She pointed at his coffee, the third refill she'd gotten for him. "Drink that before it gets cold. I hope my assistance today was helpful."

He sent her off with a grunt that seemed to pass as "good job."

After depositing the laptop in her room, and reviewing the documents that contained her new identity, her next stop was Beatrice's office.

She didn't burst in this time, going through the chain of command and waiting until Connor, Beatrice's office manager, told her she could enter.

Inside, the head of SFI motioned her to a chair.

"I need an office," Vivi said.

Although she hadn't offered to talk to Sloane, Beatrice instantly sat up straighter. "The only one I have empty isn't much. At the new SFI, things will be—"

Vivi stopped her with a raised hand. "I'm not staying with you permanently. I'm doing this for Sloane, and for you, but no one else, are we clear?"

Beatrice's lips quirked as if hiding a smile. "Whatever you want." She stood and grabbed her cell. "Let's go see your office."

She was right, it wasn't much, but the corner work-space had a window overlooking the street and a door she could close when necessary. Good enough. "Needs paint, a desk, and a file cabinet."

At Beatrice's request, Connor had accompanied them. He tapped on his computer tablet. "What color, what type, and what size?"

Vivi imagined herself in the space, the way it would look inside her mind palace. "Pine green, a corner desk with lots of drawers, preferably white and as big as you can get." She didn't even know what that would be used for, but it would seem familiar, and maybe the set up would trigger her brain to remember that day.

"Roger that," he said, and with a nod from Beatrice, turned to go.

"One more thing," Vivi called after him. "I want a nice espresso machine, and a set of mugs. Nothing skimpy. Diner size with good handles."

He disappeared and she and Beatrice strolled around the small space. "Do you need a couch, or a couple visitor chairs?"

Nice try. She was not going to get sucked into seeing patients. "No, but I would appreciate one of those play-mats, like you have in your office. Construction paper, crayons, a few new toys that Sloane hasn't seen before. Dolls that resemble you, Cal, and her."

Beatrice peered out the door, as if she wished Connor would return and make a new list. "I'm sure that can be arranged."

"I'm going to ask things of you that you're not going to like."

Beatrice returned her attention to Vivi. "Like what?"

Parents were usually the reason children were

screwed up. Didn't take a Ph.D. to know that. "Have you considered that it's something you or Cal are doing that is causing these nightmares?"

"Of course. I have a daily tracker and I keep account of everything she is exposed to so we can compare that to when she has them."

"Good. I'd like to see those records." She studied a scuff mark on the wall, scrutinized the ceiling. She could hang a bird cage from it, or get a standing one. "I assume Cal suffers from PTSD, as do many of your employees." She was still considering going to that peer support group meeting. Processing what had happened to her in prison was going to take time, and while she was no hero like he and the others, being able to share her story with them might help. "Is it possible he's had an episode that scared her?"

Beatrice's face blanched. "Cal would never hurt our daughter."

"I believe you, but it's one of the ugly areas I have to look into. If you want answers, Beatrice, I have to explore every possible avenue."

The rigid shoulders softened. "I know."

"I'll need to see the personnel files of all those who have regular contact with Sloane. Bring her by first thing tomorrow. In the afternoon, we're having a group meeting in your office. You, Cal, and anyone else who is close to Sloane."

"I'll rearrange schedules and make sure everybody attends. As long as we are addressing uncomfortable subjects, you need to see Cassandra Donovan, my chief operating officer. She'll have paperwork for you to sign.

Nothing like what you did with NSA, but a few legal documents. The standard."

The thought made Vivi itch. She glanced out the window, grateful that it was coated with a reflective film that kept anyone from seeing her. She craved light, yet felt too exposed to go outside. "Is there a reason I don't have a pointman?"

Another inquiry Beatrice was not expecting. "If you have questions, you know you can come to me."

She pivoted slowly and sat on the dusty window ledge. "I have a lot of damn questions, and unfortunately, neither you, nor anyone else here, has the answers. You can tell me this, why did you recruit Lt. Commander Kincaid?"

"Why are you using his former rank to refer to him?"

A question for a question. Fair enough. "Addressing him as 'Mr. Kincaid' seems wrong."

Beatrice seem to smother an eye roll. "I didn't recruit him. He came to us after you were declared dead. Whoever sent him to drug you and sneak you out of Lawrence's camp didn't tell him you survived. They let him think he'd killed you. I suspect they didn't want him tracking you to that black site and busting you out."

"They tried to use that as leverage, in fact, to get me to talk. The agony of knowing a SEAL like him believes he killed you when you're actually still alive is pretty damn good torture. Unfortunately, I literally could not tell them what they wanted to know, and the truth is, they would've killed me anyway, if I had. But *you* knew I was alive."

"He didn't take it well that I didn't tell him before sending him in."

Ian had always been cold steel under those intense

green eyes and fiery Irish spirit. "You believe letting him rescue me will bring him some kind of peace? I've got news for you, I'm pretty sure he hates me right now, because he still assumes I'm a traitor."

Beatrice appeared mildly amused. "I sent him on this assignment because he had the skills. He refused body-guard work and I didn't want his first job for us to be in the field on an undercover mission, since his last went side-ways with you. Eventually, he might be a good operative again, but if he chooses not to test those waters, there are other positions available. Your exfiltration was a straight-forward in-and-out. I knew he could handle it."

"Pretty words, and I don't doubt that your strategic mind did, indeed, decide that was the best option, but I don't believe you. You're playing psychologist, thinking that breaking me out will fix the trauma he went through believing he killed me."

"Not to mention the fact that he married you, and he's been beating himself up for not keeping you safe in the first place."

Vivi went very still. They'd kept their marriage a secret, planning to reveal it when they felt safe. Had Ranger spilled the beans after she called him husband the night of the rescue? "Why would you think we're married?"

"Dr. Montgomery," Beatrice emphasized the moniker, "I know everything about you, except the reason you went to Berlin six months ago. It makes no difference to me, but you must've been trying to contact Ian. For you to take that risk, and possibly blow his cover, is completely unlike you, so I assume it was a life and death matter. Only you know the truth. I'm no matchmaker, but the way that man looks at you? He's still very much in love."

The hits just kept coming. She wanted to cover her belly with her hands, but she forced them to stay by her side. Never show weakness, it was something she learned in prison. "You are one of the most intelligent people I've ever met." Vivi moved away from the window. SFI was probably more secure than NSA headquarters, but she suddenly felt vulnerable. Exposed. "But let's get something straight. Nobody outside of this room can ever know that about him and me. Mick Ranger already does and that's not good. The marriage was a mistake. I want your word, Beatrice. Absolutely no one. It could put him at risk."

"How do you know?"

She didn't, but everything felt dangerous right now. "Deductive reasoning. Like you said, I would never have gone to Lawrence and risked exposing Ian if it hadn't been a life and death situation. I just don't remember the specifics."

Beatrice headed for the exit. "I won't say anything, but you need to talk to Ian. He might have the key to unlock the memory."

The clamp around her lungs was back. *That's what I'm afraid of.*

But fear had no place in her life anymore. Gritting her teeth, she straightened her spine and went to confront him.

EIGHT

Ian sat on his bed trying to match his clean socks. Like the images and thoughts in his head, nothing seemed to line up.

A knock sounded on his door, and he didn't look up, determined to find the missing black calf sock he needed in the pile of other black socks. "Yeah," he grumbled.

For a heartbeat, nothing happened, and then the door swung open slowly and a shadow fell across the floor. He rifled through the pile and *bingo*. The little bastard had been hiding. "There you are."

"I'm not a traitor."

At the sound of her voice, he jerked, coming to his feet as if his CO had walked in. The unruly socks fell to the floor.

Vivi stood there, backlit from the hall's illumination, hands balled into fists. "I still haven't remembered why I went to Berlin and willingly walked into Lawrence's compound, but it wasn't to betray my country. *Our country.*"

Snatching up the socks, he threw them on the mattress. That's what they'd branded her, but he'd never really believed it. Even though all the evidence suggested otherwise.

And he liked empirical evidence. He needed things to be straightforward, for facts to line up. To be able to take the macro—the big picture—and pick it apart and analyze it down into the micro. He searched for patterns. For things to make sense.

Nothing about his wife made sense.

Moving his rucksack and boots off the single chair, he motioned her in. "Why don't you have a seat?"

She bit her bottom lip, staring at the seat and shifting her weight from one foot to the other. Seeing her uneasy and unsure made his chest squeeze. Genevieve Montgomery had never been unsure a day in her life. What had prison done to her?

What had *he*?

"I don't want to bother you." She still wouldn't meet his eyes. "Beatrice knows about...us. Ranger too. I'm going to ask Rory to make our marriage certificate disappear. I just wanted you to know, so you don't have to worry about that anymore."

Everything inside him seized up. "Why would you do that?"

She took a deep breath and paused, seeming to get her thoughts in alignment. "Technically, the world believes I'm dead, so you're free, but I don't want our...indiscretion in Vegas to cause blowback on you. I know you're no longer with the military, but you don't want to be the husband of a traitor, regardless."

She looked small standing there. Breakable. Her voice was too quiet, too disheartened. He wanted to reach out and take her in his arms, tell her that it would all be okay, but she wasn't the same person he'd known previously, and he honestly had no evidence that things would ever be okay between them again.

"You're not a traitor, and I don't care about the marriage license. I mean..." That had come out wrong. "I care about *you*, not about what other people think. I would like a few answers, but I heard what you told Beatrice. Trauma can do that—make you close off certain memories. When your mind believes you're ready to handle it, you'll uncover them. You just need time."

Who was the psychologist here, he wondered.

Her face was in shadow, but he saw the corners of her pretty eyes soften slightly. "You deserve a life, and I know you've found one here. I'm staying to help Sloane, if that's possible, but after that, I'm undecided. My new identity as Vivian Greene is still malleable according to Rory, and I can decide on my backstory once I figure a few things out. Meanwhile, I won't interfere with your future. I want you to be happy, and I won't hang around here longer than necessary."

She turned and fled before he could find the words to respond, and even though she hadn't entered the room, it suddenly seemed too bare, too stark, without her. Even in the shape she was in, a shadow of her former self, her unique personality influenced any space she came in contact with.

His natural instinct was to go after her, but she was like a frightened animal right now. Underneath it, he knew she was still strong, determined, but he needed to use kid gloves to convince her that her future was with him.

Fighting his instinct to chase her down, he told himself it was progress that she had come to him and initiated conversation. He would have his chance to prove to her that he wasn't going anywhere. He would apologize for calling her a coward.

He would get the answers he needed, and maybe she would as well, but he'd always known they were better together than apart.

All he had to do was convince *her* of that.

During his years in the military, he'd faced some pretty big challenges. Helping her uncover the truth of that night and stopping her from throwing away their marriage might be the biggest and most important one yet.

Leaving the unmatched socks, he went to see Rory. The IT guy was not in his normal spot, but working on his physical therapy downstairs next to the gym. Normally, Ian wouldn't have interrupted, but this was important.

He approached Rory and Dr. Amelia Thorpe, the physical therapist. "I need to talk to you in private."

Dr. Thorpe gave him the evil eye. "Can't it wait?"

Rory grunted as he did another leg curl. "What do you want, Kincaid?"

"It's about a personal matter. You're going to get a request from"—he stopped himself from saying her name, or giving away any details. "Um... Someone is going to ask you to delete something that..."

Shit. This was touchy business, and he didn't need the physical therapist suspecting there was anything going on between him and Vivi. If it were up to him, he would get on the PA system and announce to everyone that they were married, but his wife had never been demonstrative, and he wasn't going to undermine her in anyway. He would convince her he still loved her and wanted to stay married. Or get married again, due to the circumstances. Her being dead to the world had advantages, but also had little things like this they would have to work around. He didn't care. He would do it, whatever it took, to bring back the woman he'd known. To make her feel loved again, supported again. When she was ready, then he'd announce it from the tree tops.

"Spit it out, rookie," Rory growled. He finished his rep and grabbed the nearby towel to wipe sweat from his neck. He started to growl something else, then saw the consternation on Ian's face. "Oh, *that*." He glanced at Thorpe. "I know I'm a pain in the ass, but could you give me a minute with him?"

Hands on hips, she rolled her eyes. Her black hair was braided and hung down over one shoulder. She flipped it to her back and gave him a scolding look. "One minute. That's it, Then we're back to it."

She was a petite thing, but when she stomped away, she seemed three times larger. Rory chuckled. "I like her."

By the look in his eyes, there was more than *like* going on here. "I'm glad the therapy is working for you. I'm a jerk to interrupt, but I just found out,"—he lowered his voice—"Vivi plans to ask you to find our marriage certificate and delete it. Don't."

He wiped his face. "Did you woo her with your charm and cause her to have a change of heart?"

"Something like that." At least that was the plan.

"If she asks, I'll put a pin in it for twenty-four hours, but no longer."

"Dude, I thought we were friends."

"I like her better." He shrugged. "What can I say?"

Bastard. "Forty-eight hours. I need time to make her feel safe again."

Rory sighed with the dramatic flair a Hollywood actress would envy. "Fine, rookie. Forty-eight. Just don't come on too heavy and piss her off, okay? I don't want to lose my new assistant."

"Not a rookie." He started walking backward, trying to keep his grin hidden. "I owe you, man. Thanks."

"Be good to her or I'll kill you in your sleep."

Ian saluted him. The man had performed plenty of wet work for the CIA, doing exactly that. "Roger that."

NINE

The next few days went by quickly, the hours filled with research into child psychology, coming up with a treatment plan for Sloane, and avoiding Ian.

Sessions with Sloane were fun, filled with simple things, like coloring and playing with dolls. She kept them short, and invited Maggie to them as well. The dog was a natural at playing therapist. More than once, all three of them had taken a short nap on the mat.

She almost felt normal, which was one of the reasons she was steering clear of Ian. She'd said her peace, and she meant every word.

When not working on Sloane's treatments, Rory kept her busy combing databases, finding connections here and there for different "persons of interest" as he called them. Financial records, vacations in exotic places, layers of shell companies—anything that might tie one entity to another. Even whether they used the same cleaning service or real estate guru. He was particularly interested in the terrorist group 12 September, but worked on that himself.

Vivi understood the human brain and how people thought, the relationships it built and protected. The motivations that drove folks. Rory often asked her random questions about such, trying to learn more about those he hunted. He might have given up wet work, but he still thought like a predator.

She'd read over the classified reports on the laptop, filling in most of the blacked out terms and names. For all intents and purposes, it appeared she'd gone of her own accord to Berlin and made some kind of deal with Lawrence. A deal that had labeled her a traitor to her country.

All the sensitive information in her head, all the details of missions that her clients had shared, their very names, ranks, and skill sets, made her a threat should she take any of it public or sell it to the highest bidder. She was a walking, breathing threat to the U.S., and blowing the whistle on any of the alphabet agencies, or offering a trade with a terrorist, was certainly grounds for immediate elimination.

Yet, Lawrence was still walking around a free man, and had done nothing out of the ordinary—there'd been no increased attacks on any American bases, no spies or special op soldiers' identities revealed, nor anything suggesting the man had received intel from her.

More than ever she was determined to figure it out. Her next step was to research what Ian and his SEAL team had been doing that weekend. Had she known he was supposed to be there? If so, how?

Today, however, she was in her office and staring at the dozens of paint chip cards Sabrina had thrown on her desk.

"I'm sorry," the woman said, fingering them, and then her ponytail. "I know Connor told me the color you wanted, but all I could remember was that it started with an M, and he's in a team meeting, so his phone is off. It's protocol. I figured I'd grab all the ones that fit." She smiled and tapped a brightly colored card. "Magenta is probably not it, right? I should have left that at the store, but Marigold is pretty. Oh, and how about these... Mardi Gras? Magic Mint? Here's my favorite—Misty Rose. I mean, obviously I love Maximum Red"—she flipped her ponytail—"but not on walls."

Her face was so expectant and so...worried, Vivi pretended to study each of her suggestions. "Very pretty, yes. You have a great eye for color. I think I like this one." She held up May Green. A touch brighter than Ian's eyes, but perfect for a single wall. The room was too small for too much color, but it definitely needed some.

Sabrina inclined her head. "That's nice. Spring like. A fresh start. I'll run back and get a few gallons." A hand barely grazed her belly. "And some Misty Pink."

Vivi hated to be waited on, but the thought of going to the home improvement store on her own made her sick to her stomach. "Just a gallon for me. I'm only covering that wall." She pointed across the way. Forcing herself to smile, she said, "I can come with you, if you want."

Sabrina glanced at the mat in the corner. "Beatrice said you were too busy to be running errands, and it's not a problem. I love the home improvement store. Connor and I are fixing up our apartment and I have so many ideas."

"You don't live on-site?"

"He did for a while, but we found this cute place, and well, you know. We're a couple and we need *alone* time." She winked and that hand ghosted over her torso again. "You know, I could get a stencil and we could put a design on your focal wall. Maybe a mirror over here, create a reading nook, a few candles. Warm the place up, you know?"

"I bet you love HGTV, don't you?"

"Is it that obv?" She looked embarrassed. "Sorry. Decorating, painting, fixing up old furniture...it's so different than my work in the lab. It's tactile and" —she rubbed her finger and thumb together— "real. Not numbers and quantities and percentages."

"Balance. Using both sides of your brain. It's healthy."

She snapped her fingers. "Exactly. I'm creating rather than simply analyzing."

"Let's wait on the stencil and reading nook for the time being. I'm not sure how long I'll be around." She wondered what it might feel like to fix up an apartment, to be expecting a baby. They probably hadn't told anyone yet, and Vivi worked hard at not staring at Sabrina's belly or giving away that she knew. "I don't want to spend a bunch of Beatrice's money on my office."

"I get that." She narrowed her brown eyes. "You're not psychoanalyzing me right now, are you?"

Busted. "What would make you think I am?"

"You're studying me. It's probably automatic, isn't it? You do it without even realizing it."

"Are you analyzing me and this room like you would in the lab?"

"Not quite the same."

"Isn't it?" Vivi sat back. "I observe human nature because it fascinates me, but I don't build a profile of everyone I meet." Not anymore. "Your quirks, secrets, and skeletons are safe from me."

"Cool." The woman practically bounced as she turned for the door, not grasping that Vivi meant a specific secret. That was perfectly fine. "I'll round up some folks to help us paint when I get back."

"I can handle it," Vivi assured her.

"You're part of the team, now, Doc." Sabrina's voice echoed to her from the hall. "We work together in this place."

Vivi shut her laptop, thinking about what she'd read in the files of the folks who had the most interaction with Sloane. Staring at the playmat, she considered the fact that she still had absolutely no clue about the girl's nightmares. One of the books on dreams had a dozen sticky notes in it and she reread the specific sections that had stood out to her regarding children.

A knock startled her and she glanced up to find three people crowding the doorway. One was a tall, buff guy, the woman next to him was Savanna Bunkett, the investigative reporter, and the third was another woman, who favored Savanna.

The man leaned in slightly. "Hey, there. Are we disturbing you?"

Instantly wary of the TV reporter, Vivi closed her

book and put on her neutral face. "Is there something I can help you with?"

"I'm Trace Hunter, and this is my wife, Savanna Bunkett." He pointed to the other woman but before he could say anything, she volunteered her name.

"I'm Savanna's sister, Dr. Parker Jeffries. We haven't had a chance to welcome you to SFI, and just wanted to—"

Savanna pushed past both of them and smiled warmly, extending a hand. "We've heard so much about you from Beatrice. It's an honor to meet you."

Vivi had experienced so little human touch since everything had gone to hell, she hesitated before shaking. "I've seen your show. You certainly know how to get to the bottom of things."

Parker laughed and Trace snorted. "That's putting it mildly," Savanna's sister said. "Don't worry, she knows you're off limits."

Once in National Intelligence, Parker was a cognitive scientist who'd studied the brains and behaviors of terrorists. "You're the doctor involved in the Project 24 trials."

Trace flinched and the Parker looked slightly embarrassed. "I've put that behind me, but it follows me, no matter how hard I try to get away from it. I've read your papers on treating PTSD with a combination of hypnotherapy and virtual reality reprogramming. I'm quite fascinated with the neuroscience field. If you'd ever consider letting me pick your brain, I'd like to offer some of our employees the option to try a version of Trident."

They were sucking her in, bit by bit. Vivi smiled politely, reaching for some version of "no way in hell" that wasn't bitchy. She started to say something, stopped, started again.

"Why don't you come for dinner next week?" Savanna asked. "We can get to know one another and you and Parker will have time to chat."

The thought made her stomach tense. "I'm sure that would be lovely, but..."

"You need time to think about it." Trace motioned for the women to move toward the door. "Absolutely. No pressure. See you at the meeting."

It was time for her group analysis of those who spent the most time with Sloane. Trace was one of them. "I'll be there shortly."

Breathing a sigh of relief once they'd left, she shook herself. *What is wrong with me?* She had to get over this phobia of talking to people again, going places. This building, while offering a refuge, was becoming a crutch.

She'd worry about that later. Closing up her office, she headed to Beatrice's.

The group was all accounted for and waiting when she arrived. Sloane was absent, but Maggie was at Cal's feet, and Vivi took a moment to pet her.

Therapy animals... She thought about her birds. Beatrice had said she'd get them back for her. *I should include animals in my Trident—*

Stop it! No more Trident. That was over and done.

Beatrice sat next to Cal, the two holding hands. "Not to rush you," he said, glancing at his watch. Not as showy as Rory's but still what she'd expect for a military guy to sport. "I have shooting practice in twenty."

Did the man ever slow down? Those peer support

meetings might be helping him, but he was wound tighter than she was. "This won't take long." She took the only empty seat, nodding at Trace, Jax, and Connor. These were the people, along with Beatrice, who hung out with Sloane the most? Vivi opened the spiral notebook she'd brought and wrote the date at the top and the list of names. She didn't know their codenames, so she used her own method—Beatrice was Bee 1, Cal, Stressball Dog, etc. For each, she gave them a descriptive word, color, and or number. "Thank you for meeting with me today. As you know, I'm looking into possibilities to resolve Sloane's nightmares. Can any of you think of a reason she might he struggling?"

As a unit, they shook their heads.

"Okay, let's back up. I know each of you have experienced traumatic events, as children and adults. I'm sure you all understand the connection between those and challenges you have currently. For instance, my father was a genius at physics, but he wasn't good at relationships. We had a rocky one, and it still affects those I have today in some ways. I continue to have hang-ups and triggers. You do, as well, and some of your experiences may show up in your dreams also, right?"

As if they were puppets on strings, they nodded in unison.

"As adults, you have resources available to you to help you work through them. Sloane does not. Something has embedded itself in her subconscious and is trying to work its way out. That's why I'm digging into this more deeply with each of you. I don't need you to bare your soul, but I do need you to be honest with me. What traumas have you experienced during the time you've known Sloane?"

Jax sat forward, elbows on his knees. His white doctor's coat was unbuttoned and rippled with the movement. "You think we're causing her nightmares?"

"I'm simply trying to rule out the obvious." One of Vivi's play sessions with Sloane had revealed that the girl considered her stuffed animals and dolls her friends, along with the men and women of SFI. To an extent, that was fine, but she needed interaction with other children. "How often does she play with kids her age?"

A concerned frown creased Beatrice's forehead. "Once a month, maybe?"

Vivi made a note. "So, her main interaction is with adults."

"We're not exactly *normal*." Cal made air quotes as he said the word. "Our ability to keep a low profile and stay under the radar is our foremost goal. You understand that, right? Sloane isn't like other kids. We can't send her off to daycare, or allow her to have friends here for sleepovers."

Vivi bit her tongue. She didn't need to tell him how unhealthy that was for a growing child. "Does she ever do things such as go to the park?"

She knew the answer before Beatrice shook her head. "We restrict her access to public places so she doesn't become a target."

"It would be wise to find a compromise. I noticed at the compound you were installing playground equipment, and that's good, but we need to find a way to have her spend time with peers." She tapped her notepad with the pen and looked around the circle, meeting each of their gazes. "None of you answered me about any challenging experiences or traumas you've had since she was born. In the past three years, none of you have had a security client who gave you trouble? A mission that went wrong?"

They glanced at each other, and Trace spoke first. "Sure. Our jobs are challenging on a daily basis."

"Did any of these incidents directly involve the girl?"

They shook their heads and murmured "nos." Again, like a unit who lived, worked, and breathed teamwork.

Then Connor said, "Except her birth."

Vivi raised a brow. "What happened?"

"We were attacked. An art thief, seeking revenge for the death of her father and brother," Beatrice told her. "She tried to kill us."

"*During the birth?*" Vivi knew her eyes were round with shock. She'd heard impossible stories from the various men and women she'd counseled in her time, but this might top them all. "What in the world...?"

Between Cal, Beatrice, Trace, and Connor, who'd been with them when it went down, she heard a truly disturbing scenario. They were all lucky to be alive, including the precious little girl.

When they finished with the details, Vivi sat motionless for a moment. She needed to write down the facts, toy with theories, but she simply sat and let it sink in.

Jax kicked back in his chair. He seemed to know what she was thinking concerning the child's subconscious. "She was a newborn. She can't possibly remember any of that."

Vivi closed her notebook. "While it's true that most of us don't consciously recall anything from our initial two to three years of age due to a phenomenon called infantile amnesia, research suggests traumatic births increase anxiety, hyper-vigilance, and early childhood development issues. Remembering the details isn't the issue, it's the emotional trauma you and she experienced. There's nothing more frightening than your child being threatened, and during birth... Well, I can't imagine anything more traumatic for you *and* her."

Beatrice rubbed her temple. "We've screwed her up, haven't we?"

Cal patted her back. "It's my fault, not yours."

"It's not about placing blame." Vivi hated the fact they had been through something so awful, but at least she had a possible cause. She wouldn't rule out others, but a spark of eagerness replaced the previous hopelessness. "Now we know where to start rebuilding her confidence and feelings of security."

"How?" Cal asked.

Vivi stood and smiled. It felt good to be helping someone again. "I'll see both of you in my office at nine tomorrow morning."

Beatrice rose too. "With Sloane?"

"No. We start with the two of you. Neither of you sought counseling afterwards, did you?"

The couple shared a contrite glance before returning their attention to her.

"I didn't think so. You can't help Sloane work through the subconscious anxiety about what happened until you work through your own." She tipped her chin to the others. "Thank you for your help."

Feeling energized, she laid out a treatment plan in her

head for the entire family as she made her way to her office. *I'm back, baby.*

Not that she had any intention of becoming a full-blown psychologist again, but helping the girl gave her purpose.

For now.

She hummed as she let herself into her office, and came to an abrupt stop when she saw who sat in her chair.

Ian, ankles crossed on top of her desk, looked her over from head to toe. "We need to talk."

TEN

Vivi wore a slight smile that disappeared the moment she saw him. She froze, then proceeded to close the door quietly. "You're in my seat."

"You don't have any visitor chairs, or a sofa like you did in your previous office." He motioned around the room. She had no doubt done it intentionally, so people didn't sit and stay. "It's pretty stark, even for you."

Her steps were clipped as she came around to his side of the desk, knocking his feet off and grabbing him by the shirt. She jerked him out of her seat and when he planted his boots and remained rooted in her way, she glared at him. "You're right. We do need to talk. Maybe you should go get a chair. Unless you wish to sit on the playmat."

Suggesting that he was a child? It wouldn't be the first time. It had always been a good natured poke, though, and he wondered if a bit of the old Vivi was surfacing. He guessed the only reason she was agreeing to the talk was to trick him into getting said chair, just so he would vacate her space. "Only if you come with me."

She set her notebook on the desk and leaned a hip against it. "I need to know why you were in Berlin."

Going right for the main event. Typical. He probably would need that chair, because it was not a short story, but then again, the fact she was willing to discuss it was progress.

If he left to get a seat, he might miss his opportunity. He leaned against the edge of the desk, mirroring her stance. "My team was there to capture a terrorist. You probably guessed that."

She tapped the closed laptop. "I've gleaned a few details from the files Rory shared, although not the name of that terrorist. That might help me remember why I was there."

He'd considered the same thing. Was it possible she'd learned something about their target in Berlin from another operative she counseled? Perhaps even from a staff member who came to see her for therapy? It might explain everything. "Cesar Alon. Ring any bells?"

Her brows knit. "The Filipino drug lord?"

He nodded. "Counterintelligence escalated his network, which included Jim Lawrence, to an APT." An advanced persistent threat, as classified by the CIA and Homeland, didn't typically call for Ian's team, yet one of the powers that be had decided to chase Alon. "We were to apprehend him the night you walked into that party and blew our mission."

"You were on the inside of Lawrence's network. How?"

Interesting story, that. "While doing surveillance on Alon, I was approached by a man who thought I was someone else—one of Lawrence's insiders. Goes by the name Jack Spear. Spear is a...what's the term?" He snapped his fingers. He was a SEAL, not a spy. "A guy who sells fake information for political gain or money. You know, he spreads propaganda for the drug lords and cartel leaders."

"A fabricator?"

"That's it. Spear is a fabricator for Lawrence. He was supposedly out of town and not attending that party, which was a cover for a meeting with several other crime bosses, like Alon. We had planned to secretly infiltrate the house, kidnap the Filipino, and be gone without anyone noticing his disappearance. When the man accosted me and acted like I was Spear, saying he thought I was out of town, we figured it was a good way for me to pinpoint our target and get him out with less risk. So we worked on a plan, and I managed to score an invite to the party. And then you showed up."

She twisted her lips to one side, thinking, analyzing. He could see the gears turning in her head, going over those names, trying to access her memories of that night. She gently pushed him out of the way and sat. "Why did you have the drugs to knock me out? Were they for Alon?"

"Didn't expect him to come along peacefully. I was to go in, get him alone, inject him, and haul his ass out of the compound with the help of my team."

"They were watching the guests I assume, and spotted me. They alerted their superiors, who alerted NSA."

"They had to. We had no idea what you were doing

there, but we assumed they had sent you. My CO was pissed because nobody had warned us a U.S. civilian with top-secret clearance was going to be walking into that event."

Her eyes hardened and her face went stoic. "I sure threw a kink into everything, didn't I? You ended up having to take me out, instead of Alon, because they thought I'd turned traitor."

He placed his hands on the desktop, staring down into her eyes. "The only thing I assumed was that you could be in great danger if Lawrence figured out who you were and what you knew."

She leaned back in her chair, not liking the fact he'd invaded her personal space. Her gaze cut to the window. "I *am* sorry, you know."

He clenched his jaw, needing to tell her that he forgave her, but he wasn't sure exactly what he was exonerating her for. The fact she'd screwed up his mission? Cost him Alon? Betrayed her country?

Betrayed me? "I've spent the past six months trying not to love you."

Her focus snapped back to him. "Did it work?"

God help him. "No."

Her throat worked as she swallowed. "I'm sorry for that as well."

Why? Because she didn't love him anymore? For once, he wished he could climb inside her brain and understand her better. "Do you know how hard you fought me that night?"

Her eyes widened. "I fought you?"

He nodded. "You were...different. I tried to talk to you,

find out why you were there, but you seemed totally detached, like you didn't even know me. My hair was long and I wore a beard, but seriously, you didn't recognize me, and tried to take me out when I insisted you leave with me. That's why I had to resort to the injection. I didn't want to. You honestly don't remember punching me in the face?"

Shock showed in her expression. "I would *never* do that." She shook her head in dismay. "Why was I there?"

"That's what we have to figure out. Do you still think it had to do with my mission to grab Alon?"

She shrugged and threw her pen down. "During my debriefing, they never gave me a chance to figure it out. I told him I couldn't remember, so they assumed I was lying and that I had gone to the other side. One of my interrogators tried to get me to admit I was a double agent under deep cover. Can you imagine?"

He straightened. "How do we restore your memory?"

Her pause and subsequent heavy sigh suggested she wasn't happy to share. Or possibly not happy about what it would entail. "There are three major classifications of memory: sensory, short-term, and long-term. As they imply, sensory comes from the world around us, short-term involves fifteen to thirty second time spans, and long-term allows us to store information and retrieve it after longer intervals. Our working memory performs the processing of all of these, and information can be retrieved consciously or unconsciously."

He sort of followed that. "Okay, and?"

"There are two probabilities for the reason I have blocked that night—something scared me so bad that I don't want to remember it, or the drugs screwed me up.

What happened is in here"—she tapped her head—"but it's subconscious at the moment. I think hypnotherapy may be my only option to retrieve it."

A surge of expectation made him smile. She was an expert at hypnosis with her Trident therapy. "Great. Then we can get to the bottom of this."

"Potentially, yes, but don't get your hopes up."

"Why not?"

"I can't hypnotize myself, so I'll need someone who's experienced to do it, and who Beatrice will give her okay to. It can't be just anyone. I'm dead to the world, remember? If another psychologist puts me under and retrieves information that is sensitive or endangers any of us, it would put SFI, and Cal and Beatrice, in a bad situation."

He hadn't thought of that. "Can't Jax or Parker do it? They're both doctors."

She rocked in the chair, those full lips of hers working to the side once more. "Parker maybe. She's had similar training. I would need practice volunteers, though, to show her my method."

If only he could wipe the worry off her face and get that smile she'd worn earlier back. The way she gnawed her bottom lip told him how much pressure she was feeling. "You don't have to do it, you know. In the end..." Was he really about to admit this? "I don't care why you were there, and I know now you had no control over the fact they silenced you and made all of us believe you were dead." He'd just admitted he didn't care if she *was* a traitor. Holy fuck balls. He'd spent his whole life wanting to be a soldier. Then to join the SEALs. To dedicate himself to protecting those who couldn't protect themselves. "If you want to leave that buried, fine. You and I can move forward, regardless."

"I don't think so." She gave him a weak smile and his stomach fell.

"Why not?"

"Neither one of us has ever been the type to bury our head in the sand. We need to face this head on."

Oh. She wasn't telling him to get lost, that she didn't love him anymore. Only that they needed answers. Relief swamped him. She was definitely getting some of her old spunk back. "I'll help however I can. I'll recruit some of the guys to let Parker practice on them. Therapy itself is an uncomfortable thing; hypnosis is ten times worse. But I'm sure I can convince at least one or two."

She studied him for a long moment, but he refused to fidget under her stern gaze. "You told Rory to ignore my request about the marriage license."

Busted. "About that. I was going to tell you, ask you to wait a little longer before pulling the plug."

"Why?"

Hadn't he already told her? Six months of waking up every day with a knot in his gut. Six months of trying to hate her for the betrayal. She seemed to hold her breath as he found the words to say. "I know you're not the same person you were. Hell, neither am I. But we had something special, Vivi. I want to give us another try, and I hope you do, too."

Nothing changed in her expression. She seemed more curious than anything. "Ian, we barely knew each other when we took those vows. It was a fantasy, thinking we could walk away from our jobs. And after all that's happened, we certainly don't know each other now."

The words hit him like bullets, piercing his heart. "Don't know each other? Who are you trying to convince, me or you?"

"Seems like a lifetime ago, doesn't it? Our vacation in Vegas?"

She had planned to leave NSA. He was almost done with his Navy term. Together, they were going to buy a house, find regular jobs that didn't involve the government, terrorists, or keeping secrets. That imaginary family they'd talked about hovered in front of him like a mirage. "Vivi... for me, nothing has changed. I still love you."

"You seemed quite angry when you found out I wasn't dead. You thought I betrayed you, as well as our country. You can pretend otherwise right now, but I know the truth."

"I was wrong." He leaned in again, bearing down on her as he poked his chest. "I thought I'd killed you. It was grief, balled up in here."

She slowly came to her feet, once again the consummate professional. "Look, we both need therapy. We have a lot of awful stuff to work through, and we can't expect to be partners until we've confronted what happened to each of us."

"You once told me that therapy comes in many forms." He leaned closer, focusing on those beautiful lips. "How about we try things our way?"

Before she knew what was coming, he kissed her.

ELEVEN

Vivi's breath caught at the touch of Ian's warm lips. The spark he always ignited, buried deep these past few months, burst into flame, searing through her.

It was wrong, but her body didn't care. She'd had to be stone cold and unemotional for so long, it had become her armor. An armor that was melting slowly since arriving here.

Helping Sloane, finding support from the strangers that filled the halls, discovering that her husband still wanted a future with her—it had all blindsided her.

Her fingers went to his hair, the back of his head, his shoulders, as his lips parted hers. Everything inside her combusted, all the pain and suffering going up in a ball of flames.

His hands went around her waist, as her arms circled his neck, pulling him closer. He lifted her off her feet and her knees slid across the desk, sending her notebook and pen flying.

His tongue swept into her mouth and she moaned, still on her knees, and pressed herself against him. It had always been like this since that first time when they met for coffee. Even then, they'd both known the sexual heat between them could no longer be denied.

His hands brushed the bottom of her breasts through the button down shirt she wore. Their tongues did a tango, in and out, lips unable to get enough of each other.

"Vivi," he murmured in her ear. "I've missed you so much."

She'd missed him, too. God, she'd missed it all—her work, the patients, her damn birds. But her mouth couldn't form the right words to reply, her brain on hiatus as her body did the talking.

Nimble fingers unbuttoned the blouse before he grazed the tops of her breasts with his knuckles. She shifted to sit, kicking off her heels, and grabbed his belt. With trembling fingers, she started to undo it, fumbling with the leather and buckle.

He caught her by the wrists. "My place," he said on a heavy breath. "We need privacy."

No way. She couldn't wait. Her brain was screaming at her not to do this, not to go there. "Here. Now." She pushed him away. "Just lock the door."

It took mere seconds for him to dash to it and back, a knowing smirk on his face. She removed her bra and he gazed in awe at her breasts. "I've missed these beauties," he said, cupping them.

"Too much talking." She grabbed his belt and jerked it

from the loops. Then she attacked his button-fly, yanking his jeans open. *Don't do it,* her traitorous brain screamed. *Not listening,* she told it. *After all I've been through, I deserve this. Deserve to be held and made love to.* "I need you."

Once more, he took her hands, restricting her access to him. "We have plenty of time. I want to enjoy this. *You.* I never thought I'd get another chance."

His lips found hers again as he bent her back, her breasts rising. Then he kissed her jaw, her neck, nipped her earlobe. She shuddered, practically orgasmic from his simple touch.

He brought his mouth down to her breasts and she moaned again as his tongue flicked over a nipple. Taking his time, he sucked it in, still keeping her hands pinned.

Bastard. She closed her eyes and her body swayed as he worked his magic on her, but it wasn't fair. "I need..." she started, but he silenced her with a kiss.

"I know what you need." His voice was low and rasped against her skin. "Let me give it to you."

His free hand went between her legs and she gasped at the ache his fingers caused. He rubbed her through the material of her pants, and she wrapped her legs around his hips, the stroking of his thumb creating a wildfire. *Oh god.*

"Surrender," he said against her temple. "Allow yourself some pleasure."

The rhythm increased and he dipped his mouth to the other breast. She was at his mercy, completely undone. Out of control, like her life had been since that night in Berlin.

No, since the day she'd met him. Those green eyes had

sized her up the same way she had him. The stubbornness in his answers, refusing to let her into his mind until he was confident she wouldn't betray him. The teasing and sarcasm—anything he could do to get her to smile, to laugh.

He'd been so good for her, seducing her mind as well as her body.

Even now, when she shouldn't want him, shouldn't screw up his life again, he was here. He knew how to take his pleasure from her by giving her everything she needed. "Please," she panted, so close to the first climax she'd enjoyed in months. "Let me touch you."

In an instant, he released his grasp. Her right hand went to his erection, straining against his underwear. Her left tangled in his hair and she arched against him.

He swore on a growl when she gripped him through the soft cotton and moved with the same rhythm as he was using on her. Take her time? *Puulease.* She needed him and she needed him *now.*

There was too much material between them but she couldn't hold on any longer. He kissed her deeply and on the next stroke of his thumb, she shattered. Her fingers flew to his shoulders, her back bowing at the intensity of it. She dug her nails into his back. "*Ian!*"

Her voice echoed in the room. He held her, letting her ride it out. Chest heaving, she clung to him, the floaty buzz of the aftermath making her sway again. He dotted her face and neck with kisses, and as her world once more righted itself, she licked her lips, opened her eyes and sighed deeply. "Damn. I needed that."

A smug grin curved his lips. "We're just getting started."

She reached for him again, shoving the cotton aside to get to his velvet skin. It was his turn to gasp as she gave his thick erection a tug. "Now you're at *my* mercy."

A knock made her jump, and he barked a curse.

"Dr. V?" Sabrina's voice cut through the door. "You okay in there? I brought the paint and a few hands to help with the walls."

"Shit," Ian swore under his breath, backing out of Vivi's grip and hurriedly shoving his cock inside his pants. "What's she doing here?"

Timing was everything, wasn't it? "I'm good," Vivi called, her voice husky. "Can we do this another time?"

"Um, I guess." The woman sounded stunned. "It's just that we're all here and it won't take long."

If she sent Sabrina and the others away, they might not come back. "Looks like we're having a painting party," she murmured to Ian. "Hand me my bra." He did and as she put it on and adjusted her breasts, she saw him watching. She gave him an incredulous look.

"We aren't done," he said, tweaking her nipple through the material. He gave her an evil smile that sent that flame bursting to life inside her again.

Hurriedly, she jumped off the desk, accepting her shirt from him before he retrieved the notebook and pen off the floor. "Give me a minute," she told Sabrina, feeling her face flush.

Using her fingers, she combed her hair and faced him, buttoning the blouse. "How do I look?"

"Beautiful," he said, chuckling as he reached for her

buttons. She'd done them up wrong and his nimble fingers fixed them in a heartbeat.

"Not a word of this to anyone," she admonished.

"Of course not," he said with a grin that suggested he planned to tell the world.

Ignoring him, she drew a deep, steadying breath and unlocked the door.

TWELVE

Ian leaned against the desk, watching her let the others in. He'd done it—brought back that rare smile to her lips. For the first time since he'd seen her in that prison cell, there was color in her cheeks, a bounce in her step.

As the volunteers filed in, there were a lot of looks thrown around. At Vivi, at him, and then between those in the group. It wasn't hard to figure out what he and his wife had been doing before they'd interrupted.

Sabrina had recruited Ranger and Zeb. The instant Vivi spotted the former spymaster, she brightened even more. They'd obviously crossed paths at some point in her career, and Zeb accepted her hug with a pat on the back, acting as though he was embarrassed by her show of affection.

"I thought you were dead," she said, shifting back and looking him over. Her voice had a note of teasing in it.

"I like it that way." He rubbed her head with his

knuckles. "Prison doesn't suit you, Doc."

"It sucked."

He ran his hands down her thin arms and wrinkled clothes, sliding his eyes to Ian and back to Vivi. "How you gettin' on?"

"Better now that I'm *not* dead," she answered with a dry snicker. "I had no idea you were part of the Cult of Beatrice."

He chuckled and winked at her. "All the best folks are."

Sabrina tossed down tarps and a bag of brushes, towels, and blue tape. Mick hauled two gallons of paint to a corner of the room. "Gonna need a ladder," he said, surmising the height of the ceiling.

Vivi pointed at the hall. "I'm going to put on some old clothes. Be right back."

Ian boosted himself off the desk, his gaze locked on her backside. "I need to change, too."

"Sure you do," Mick said with a cunning tone in his voice. "Go take care of your woman. We've got this."

He was going to take care of her all right. Ian left the smirks and knowing glances of the others behind and raced after his wife.

He heard the ding of the elevator around the corner and picked up his pace.

Wife. He loved the term. Never thought he'd have one. A year ago, he hadn't even wanted a long-term commitment. His career had been everything. He'd loved the military, loved the discipline as well as the adventure. When he'd been required by the Navy to routinely see a psychologist after every mission, he'd balked at the idea. Like most guys, the last thing he wanted to do was talk about his feelings.

And then he'd met Vivi.

The elevator doors were shutting, Vivi's eyes widening when she saw him closing in. He slipped sideways through the tight opening, caught her up and pinned her against the back wall.

She squealed and wrapped her arms around him. He ground his pelvis against her and she pressed her breasts into his chest.

It was one floor, one goddamned floor, and not nearly enough time for anything more than a kiss before the ding announced they had arrived at their destination.

He carried her out, barely noticing one of the guys take a step back to allow them to pass. Her room was too far and she was so warm, so willing in his arms. He kissed her and kissed her and kissed her.

He was never going to let her out of his sight again. Never stop touching her. Never let her go.

Kicking the door to her room open, he loved the way she laughed and then stretched herself out on the mattress once he dumped her there. "So caveman," she quipped.

"Here I thought it was romantic." He locked the door and flipped on the lamp next to the bed. She had no windows, no natural light save for a narrow bar along the south wall near the top of the room. While he didn't mind a sexy tussle in the dark, today he wanted to see every inch of her.

He planned to take his time, savor it, because it had been so long, and he'd believed for months that he would never get to touch her again.

Her eyes were pools of lust as she watched him remove his shirt and unbutton his jeans. She sat up and swung her legs over the edge, reaching for him. Her hands yanked his pants down, his erection jutting through the material of his underwear and into her face.

He would never get tired of hearing her laugh. She tugged the briefs away and took him in her mouth before the sound of it died out.

His body jerked, his hand going to the back of her head, the tickle of her hair under his palm. She clasped his ass cheeks with both hands and gorged herself on him.

"God, Vivi," he moaned, hips bucking in rhythm with her mouth. She took him deep and pressed her tongue up against the underside of his cock, increasing the sensation.

His back arched and he came in a rush, her continuing to suck every last drop out of him. His knees went weak and he could barely stand, falling onto the bed beside her when she released him.

He lay there for long moments, appreciating her fingers stroking his chest, his legs. She tugged off his boots and pants, tossing them aside.

Opening his eyes, he watched as she began a slow striptease. Once again, the blouse came off and fell to the floor. She turned her back to him and slowly peeled down her slacks inch by inch over her hips, butt cheeks, and down her legs. Bending forward, gave him the full view of her ass.

He reached out and touched her between her folds and she gasped. Then she moved barely out of reach and glanced over her shoulder at him as she dropped one bra strap, then the other down her arms.

Damn, he was hard all over again.

She strolled around the bed, and just out of reach, her eyes full of wicked delight as she watched his erection grow. She undid the bra and dropped it on his belly. "Are you sure you want this?"

"You're kidding, right?"

"Not the sex," she said, "this." Her finger waggled between them. "Us."

"Are you torturing me on purpose? You want me to beg?"

Her expression turned thoughtful and she placed a finger to her cheek as if considering it. "I do like it when you're on your knees."

He growled, sitting up and grabbing her in one swift move. She yelped like she had in the elevator, and then she was falling on him as he lay back.

Nothing about her was easy, and he didn't care. She refused to let him take his time with her, mounting him in a rush, her sweet folds wet and ready for him. As he looked up into her face, caressing her breasts, he was a goner all over again. Like he'd told her, she wasn't the same woman, yet she was still all consuming.

Moving with the fervor of a person starving for a climax, he let her ride him to the brink and drive herself over it. As she came with a gasp, squeezing around him hard and tight, he followed her over that edge and went free-falling.

Hours passed with barely a notice as they became reacquainted with each other's bodies. He'd forgotten all about painting her office until they came up for air because they were both starving.

"Shit," she said, staring at the wall clock. "Sabrina's going to kill us."

"Worth it." He yawned and trailed a finger along her ribs as she sat on the edge of the mattress putting on her bra.

"They don't have room service in this place, right?"

"Only if you're in the med ward. We have to brave the mess hall."

She cringed, rising to walk to the wardrobe and sorting through a scant amount of clothes. "How can I make it up to Sabrina and the others?"

"Don't worry about them." He tugged on his jeans and shirt. "They'll understand."

On the ride down, she pulled up her hoodie, covering her head. He said nothing, knowing it bothered her to still look like a prison inmate, even though no one here cared.

The cafeteria was fairly empty, a couple of the Rock Star security guys trading stories over energy drinks at a table in the corner. Ian didn't know them, but they exchanged nods—everyone was a brother here—and then he went to work loading up a tray with food.

Vivi kept her gaze turned from the others, grabbing a few frozen burritos and microwaving them. There was always an assortment of easy-to-make meals on hand. If you had special requests, it was up to you to buy and stock them. Anything without a name on it identifying it belonged to someone was fair game.

They'd just sat down to gorge themselves when Ian's phone rang with a text from Rory. *Come to the center. Bring Dr. Greene.*

He stared at the message for a moment, wondering if it

had something to do with his request to ignore her demand to obliterate the trail regarding their marriage. He sent a reply, asking for five minutes to eat. "Rory wants to see us."

"About what?" she asked around a spoonful of yogurt.

The app was still open and Ian watched the bubble with the dots, telling him Rory was typing. "No clue."

The bubble disappeared, then came a command. *Now.*

Great. He picked up the tray with the remnants of uneaten food. "Grab what you can. We're taking it to go."

She quizzed him in the elevator, gobbling down the rest of the yogurt before she unwrapped the still-warm burrito and dug in to that. It was good to see her eat.

"Must be about our marriage," Ian guessed, "or maybe the prison break."

Her hand holding the snack dropped and her eyes widened. "You don't think someone figured it out, do you?"

His gut tightened, but he shook his head as if unconcerned. "If they had, it would be Beatrice calling us in, not Rory."

Somewhat mollified, she returned to her food and said around a mouthful, "A mission, maybe? For the two of us?"

"Beatrice or Cal would hand out orders for that." He chucked her chin. "What kind of mission do you think they'd assign to us, anyway?"

"You doubt my field skills?"

Yes. "Of course not," he lied.

She snorted, knowing he was.

The elevator stopped and they walked into the quiet

computer hub. No one was present, except for the department head. Rory didn't so much as look up. "No food in
here, you know that."

Ian made a face and set the tray on the closest desk,
shoving an energy bar in his back pocket. Vivi hurriedly
wiped her mouth, swallowing the last bite of her burrito.
Together, they made their way past the assorted cubicles
and machines, the background hum like white noise to
Ian's nerves.

Rory had an L-shaped station with multiple monitors
and keyboards. Ian shifted one of the visitor chairs so Vivi
could sit. He stayed standing. "What's up?"

Rory hit a couple keys and raised his attention to
them. As he did so, he swung a monitor around so they
could see it. "Look familiar?"

The photo was a grainy black and white, probably
from a security camera. A man's face was caught in profile
as he entered a building on a rainy night, the lapels of a
trench coat flipped up around his neck.

Ian bent and peered at the shot. At the same time, Vivi
leaned forward, her breath hitching. "Is that...?" Her eyes
turned to him. "You?"

Distant warning bells were going off in his head. He
scanned the part of the building caught in the frame, along
with the glass entrance. It didn't look familiar. "Where
was this taken?"

Rory hit a few more keys and turned a second monitor
toward them. "The Oliver Hotel in Berlin on the night of
November eleventh last year, at 1100 hours. Ring any
bells?"

Now his stomach fell. He and Vivi stared at each other. "That's not me," Ian said. "I was..."

"In Vegas getting married?" Rory asked.

"Wait," Vivi said, coming out of the chair. "The Oliver Hotel in Berlin. That's where the chancellor was assassinated."

Rory dipped his chin. "On the night of November eleventh at midnight, and they never caught the shooter."

"Where did you get this photo?" Ian asked, eyeing his profile once more. He'd been nowhere near Berlin. He did the math, confirming it—Central European time to Pacific —he was in a Vegas chapel saying "I do" about then.

Rory leaned back, the chair squeaking in protest. "It was sent to Dr. Montgomery's private phone by an unknown number two days before she touched down in Germany and walked into Lawrence's party."

Vivi sat down hard. Ian could see the wheels turning in her head. "You accessed my records?"

Rory cracked his knuckles. "Of course."

"You shouldn't be digging around in that stuff." Her voice held clear warning. "They've probably got trackers on all of it."

"They do," he agreed, not the least bit concerned.

"Look, I know everyone here believes you're the best at what you do, but it's not worth stirring this hornet's nest."

Ian placed a hand on her shoulder. "I want to know who was impersonating me that night and why."

"So do I." Beatrice strode in and stopped at the desk. "And we're going to find out."

Vivi glanced between her and Rory, fear on her face.

"You *want* them to know you're looking into it. You want them to come after you."

"Not me," Beatrice clarified, standing over Rory's shoulder and scanning the monitor on his side. "You. I want to know why someone painted suspicion about a U.S. Navy SEAL being at that hotel on the night the chancellor was assassinated, yet it wasn't brought to anyone's attention, within our government, or in Europe."

"How do you know it wasn't?" Ian asked.

Rory sat forward, fingers flying over his center keyboard. "I've accessed records from Homeland, National Intelligence, NSA, CIA, you name it. There's not a single mention of suspicion being placed on the U.S. for the assassination. No military communications, no DOD reports. Nothing."

"But someone wanted it to look like we took out the chancellor," Beatrice said. "My guess? They wanted to use it as leverage."

Vivi came out of her chair. "Leverage to get me to turn traitor and give up national secrets."

"By impersonating me," Ian said quietly.

Beatrice and Rory nodded in synch. "Whoever did this played you, Vivi," Beatrice said. "It has to be someone who knew about you and Ian."

All eyes went to her and she walked away, pivoted, and stomped back. "That's not possible. No one knew."

"Someone did," Ian said. "When you have eliminated the impossible, whatever remains, however improbable, must be the truth. Right?"

"Yes," Beatrice said. "And we're going to figure out who."

THIRTEEN

The next morning, Vivi hung her head and tried to breathe. She'd sworn she'd never do it again. Hadn't believed she'd ever *have* to.

But here she was in the office that really wasn't hers, even though it was freshly painted and had her requested items in it, segmenting everything going on in her brain, just like her days at NSA.

She gave each issue a sticky note and smacked it down on the desk.

Ian and our marriage.

Love, sex...how could they fully commit to a relationship when there were all these unanswered questions?

The sex was incredible, always had been, but it added another layer of stickiness. She tried to visualize the two of them living a normal, married life, and couldn't. Neither of them was normal, not by a long shot. He lived for action, adventure, righting wrongs. She liked staying in her office, behind closed doors, and analyzing people. Helping them, but in a different manner than he did.

She slapped down the next sticky note: *Photo.*

Beatrice had ordered Rory to plant virtual "trip wires" for whoever might notice he'd hacked into Vivi's private phone and emails. Told him to *not* cover his tracks and plant carrots for their rabbit to follow back to them.

Stupid, in Vivi's opinion. That was a can of very dangerous snakes and once it was open, there was no stuffing them back in.

While she might be dead to the world, Beatrice claimed whoever was watching—Command & Control? A terrorist like Lawrence?—would assume Ian was the one hunting down that photo to destroy it, and they'd come after him.

Making him the target.

Vivi couldn't say she was pleased by Beatrice and Rory putting Ian in danger, but her husband had thought it a brilliant move and was, at that very moment, searching through dozens of debriefings and follow-up reports about the chancellor's assassination. Like her helping Sloane, he now had a purpose.

Another sticky note: *Sloane.*

Vivi was determined to help the girl, but with her own issues filling up her waking moments, as well as tormenting her in her dreams, how could she possibly be clearheaded enough to do right by her?

She'd already outlined questions and a plan of action to use with Beatrice and Cal, but so far, she couldn't pin either of them down to have a session. They'd both ignored the order to be in her office at nine.

Which in itself was another issue. *You can't help someone who doesn't want to be helped.* Her mentor had said it all the time.

The couple claimed ridding Sloane of her nightmares was a high priority, yet both had been avoiding her.

My memory. The next sticky note joined the others.

It wasn't enough to theorize why someone had set-up Ian, and then to not use the photo and publicly throw suspicion on him and the U.S. government. It was another to figure out why Vivi had gone to Berlin and invited herself to Jim Lawrence's party.

She needed time to think. Time to sort out her memories. She needed...

Hypnosis. She stuck the final note in the center of the others.

If she could remember her motivation for what she'd done, she could solve all of the other issues. She needed a clone of herself who understood that method of recovering memories, and could handle the highly sensitive information she might reveal.

While she was at it, she needed better clothes and decent hair.

Can't have everything.

The clothes Beatrice had given her were, well, Beatrice's. Vivi looked a clone of her in pink skirts and white blouses. While the two of them were of similar height, Beatrice filled out garments much better than Vivi did.

Scratching her head where the hair was filling in again, she eyed the bright colored slips of paper and moved them around. Moved them around again. All were equally important.

What action can I take right now? Which issue had solutions that were concrete and had immediate practical value?

Her attention landed on Ian and their marriage. That was a quagmire of emotions, and he was as bullheaded as they came. Until the situation with the photo was resolved, all she could do was go along with Beatrice's plan and protect her husband.

He'd laugh at that idea. Ian had always had such a streak of independence and confidence, he'd never allow anyone, not even her, to protect him.

But what he didn't know...

Beatrice owes me. Tit for tat. If Vivi was helping Sloane, Beatrice was going to put every safeguard in place Vivi could think of to keep that target off Ian's back.

Rising, she was about to march to Beatrice's office and inform her of that, when a knock sounded at the door. "Dr. Mont—I mean, Dr. Greene? It's me, Connor."

Quickly, Vivi snatched the notes from their places and stuck them in her top drawer. Resuming her seat, she affected an air of busyness. Old habits died hard. "Yes?"

He strode in, hands full with a mug and a plate. "Black, one sugar, and the muffin is lemon-blueberry."

She slid her laptop aside as he delivered both to her, bringing out a stack of napkins from a pocket in his cargo pants. "What's all this?"

"Beatrice said you like muffins, and Sabrina brought some for the entire office." He pointed at the treat. "If you'd prefer chocolate chip or cranberry orange, I can run back and get one for you."

The coffee teased her nostrils and she sipped. "This is

fine. Better than fine, in fact. You ever tasted prison coffee?" He shook his head and made a face. Her stomach growled. "Pray you never do. You didn't have to do this, you know."

"Your espresso machine is on order, should be here today or tomorrow. You have a lot on your plate," he said, grinning as he pointed at the giant muffin. "Literally, and figuratively. Mick told me what's it like to recover from prison life, and I want you to know, Sabrina and I are here for you. All of us are. You need anything, call me. Okay?"

Vivi broke off a piece of the muffin's top and chewed. Delicious. "She's not mad I skipped out on her yesterday?"

"Nah. She was relieved, actually."

"Why?"

"You make her nervous."

Hmm. "I don't mean to." She wondered if he knew about the baby. "Afraid it comes with the territory."

"On the other hand." He withdrew a folded slip of paper. "There are others here at SFI who would like to make an appointment to see you. Professionally."

She eyed the paper and drew back an inch. Motivation. It always came down to that. She felt a touch disappointed. "That's what this is really about, isn't it? Buttering me up with coffee and sugar in order to get me to see patients."

His fingers creased the folded edge, over and over. Apparently, Sabrina wasn't the only one who had a case of nerves around her. "I know you're not ready yet, but when you are, would you at least consider talking to them?"

Compartmentalizing wasn't the only habit that was rearing its ugly head. The tug in her solar plexus had her wiggling her fingers at him to hand over the list. "They talk, I listen. That's how it works. I may ask a few questions, but mostly it's about getting them to open up and spill whatever's buried in their subconscious."

"I get that. Every person inside these walls needs that, you know. There's no possibly or probably about it." He handed her the paper. "We need you, Doctor. I hope you'll consider picking up your practice again for all of us. I've read the data on Trident. The great results you had with it. We definitely could use that type of therapy."

She was such a sucker. Keeping her game face on, she glanced over the list, sipped her coffee, as if considering it, but not committing. "I have to get *my* head on straight first. You understand that, right? I could do more harm than good."

"Sure. Of course. Listen, if you need someone to talk to..." He let the offer hang between them.

"Do you have any experience in behavioral therapy? Hypnotizing people?"

He grinned. "I can learn. Might be a cool skill to have."

Indeed it was. "I'll consider it."

She'd no sooner shooed Connor off when Amelia Thorpe's shadow fell across the threshold. "I need to ask your opinion about Rory's progress."

Vivi held in her agitated sigh and put down her pen. It wasn't that she didn't want to chat, but she knew this pattern—if she didn't establish guidelines soon, every minute of her day would be folks dropping in. "You're his physical therapist. I'm not sure what I can offer."

"May I?" Dr. Thorpe motioned to come in. Vivi

nodded and the woman advanced to her desk, glancing around for a seat. This was why she didn't have any. She stood awkwardly, wringing her hands. "He was making great strides until a week ago. He's hit a plateau and seems reluctant to push past it."

Vivi leaned back in her chair and rocked it, just because she could. To have a nice, leather chair. A beautiful desk. These were luxuries she'd once taken for granted. Never again. "What is your opinion?"

Thorpe looked to be in her thirties with smooth taupe colored skin and dark hair that she parted in the center. She pushed up the glasses on the end of her nose, a nervous tick, Vivi guessed. "I think it's me."

Vivi cocked an eyebrow, asking a silent question.

The therapist fidgeted, worrying a ring on her middle finger. "Something has changed between us. He's always a bit gruff, but all of a sudden, he's... Well, he doesn't make eye contact, doesn't joke like he used to. It's almost as if he's forcing himself to even be in the same room with me. He told me today that he's never going to walk again and it's a waste of both our times. He won't be coming for any more sessions. I should forget about him and help the others."

You can't save someone who doesn't want to be saved. "You know of nothing specific that's caused his sudden reticence? Have you spoken to any of his friends? Beatrice? They might have insight for you."

Her eyes were sad. "Seems he's acting the same with all of them."

Letting her brain replay the conversation, as well as considering her own interactions with him, she continued to rock. "How long has he been in a wheelchair?"

"Over three years."

"How have you managed to get him on his feet?"

"Nerve stimulation, better nutrition, water therapy, weights. It's nothing unusual or different, it's that he never wanted to try before."

"What made him decide he wanted to walk now, after all this time?"

"I'm not sure. He avoided me for months after I came to work here, then he saw several of the other men recovering from injuries and getting stronger. I think it gave him hope."

Or maybe he liked the pretty therapist, and now that he was on the brink of actually regaining his freedom from that chair, he was facing a new fear—rejection. "The mind plays a huge role in recovery, whether it be from physical, emotional, or mental trauma. We believe we want something, only to hit a wall when we actually see it's a possibility. The chair may have become a crutch. It offers him a form of support, literally, and reassurance mentally."

Her brows scrunched together. "I wondered about that possibility, but surely he wants to walk again."

"Subconsciously, maybe not, so he's sabotaging himself, staying in his comfort zone."

"What should I do?"

"You can't force him to show up for therapy. Either he gets past his fear of success or he doesn't. Sounds like seeing others healing and getting stronger—getting their lives back—inspired him before. Maybe it will again."

"That's it? You're telling me to leave him alone?"

A layer of helplessness laced the therapist's words. "I know it's hard to step back and let someone work through their issues. What I'm suggesting is you use some of your other patients to motivate him again. Subtly, of course. He doesn't strike me as the type of guy who likes to be told what to do, but I bet his coworkers could get him to the gym with a bit of gloating about their own progress, sprinkled with a challenge or two."

As understanding sunk in, she smiled. "Okay. How exactly do I recruit them?"

In her line of work, she couldn't be subtle. She had to instruct her patients what to do and how to do it. "How about you let me handle it?"

Relief crossed her face. "I can't thank you enough. If there's anything I can do for you, please let me know."

"I could use some of my muscle mass back. Could you give me a set of exercises and weight training tips to do that?"

Her smile lit up her face and she snapped her fingers. "I'm on it. Meet me at the gym at four, okay?"

"Can you just give me a list?" She'd have to borrow some workout clothes. "I want to try a few on my own."

The frown appeared again. "I'm happy to walk you through them."

"I was actually planning to ask somebody else to help." She gave the doctor a sly smile.

"Ooh." Thorpe winked. "Sure, I get it. I'll email you the recommended exercises."

"Great. Do you know what Rory's favorite sport is?"

"Basketball, I think. Why?"

Of course it would be one she knew nothing about.

Maybe that could work in her favor. "There's a court downstairs, right?"

"A half court, yes." Thorpe eyed her suspiciously. "What are you thinking?"

"Just curious. I'll look for that list."

Thorpe had a spring in her step on the way out.

At least one of them was happy.

Vivi expected her day to get better when Ian showed up. He said nothing but came to her side of the desk and drew her out of the chair for a kiss.

His hands went to her waist and he crushed her against him, bending her backward as he thoroughly ravaged her mouth and swept his tongue inside to dance with hers.

They nearly ended up on the desk in various stages of undress, but her phone rang, interrupting them. "Don't answer it," he said, his lips against her neck.

She laughed low and pushed him away, even though she didn't want to. "I'm waiting on a supply of virtual reality goggles and software. That's Connor. He's probably letting me know they were delivered."

"For what?"

She answered the phone, rather than him. "Yes?" It was what she expected. "You don't have to bring them up. I'll send Ian to get them."

Her husband gave her a hound dog look. "Virtual reality, huh? Sounds like you're getting back into the swing of things."

She fixed her shirt, then his. "You sound disappointed."

He glanced away. "No, I'm glad, actually, it's just..."

She placed her hands on either side of his face and made him look at her. "Just what?"

"I thought you didn't want to stay here. Didn't want to practice professionally again."

She didn't, did she? It seemed she couldn't escape it, though. "I'm helping Sloane." And maybe Rory and those on Connor's list. "Would it bother you if I did more than that?"

He kissed her forehead. "If you want to, then I'm good with it."

His tone seemed to contradict the statement. "But?"

"Nothing." He turned away. "It's stupid."

"Hey." She caught his arm and stopped him from walking out. "It's not stupid. Tell me."

"I thought maybe we'd go somewhere, start over. Get that house we talked about. Work on a family."

Ah. "I want those things, too."

Those green eyes searched hers. "But...?"

"I have to get my memories back, figure out what happened that night. I need to clear my name. We're on the same page with that, right?"

He tugged her close again, bumping their hips together. "We are. I have a plan. Trust me, okay?"

"I do." She pushed a lock of hair out of his eyes. While hers had been shorn off, his had gotten longer. "I'm just afraid of the snakes lying in wait."

"I can, and will, handle them."

"Did you find something in those reports?"

"Not sure. I have to do some fishing."

She wasn't sure she liked the sound of that.

"Cal and Beatrice have a house not far from here," he

told her. "It's now my official residence, so if any of those snakes come crawling out of their hiding places looking for me, I'm going to be waiting for them."

Any truth is better than indefinite doubt. Another Sherlock saying Vivi had often embraced. Yet... Her body temperature dropped ten degrees. "Ian, that's incredibly—"

"Stupid?"

The world felt like an earthquake under her feet. "You're one of the most intelligent, capable people I know. I was going to say 'dangerous.'" She paced to the window. "It's also incredibly smart." She whirled to face him. "I'm going to be there with you."

"No—"

Stalking toward him, she pointed a finger at his face. "Don't even think I'm letting you do this on your own."

A muscle jumped in his jaw, then he quirked his lips. "So we're playing house?"

They were playing much more than that. "Go get my package. I have some folks to help before we catch those snakes."

FOURTEEN

A few hours later, Rory was in his usual spot when Vivi arrived with Dr. Thorpe's workout list in hand.

She made a face as she stepped off the elevator, and pursed her lips as she walked to the computer station he'd assigned her.

She set the paper on the desk. "What do you have for me today?"

He wheeled over and, nosy fellow that he was, glanced at the list. "Keep on cross-checking the numbers I gave you yesterday with the records from 12 September's file. We still need to find the connection between their movements and those bank deposits in the Cayman account."

She flopped into the chair, waking up the computer. She didn't have time for this, but he was now a patient, even though he didn't realize it. "On it."

"What's this?" he asked, pointing at the therapist's handwriting.

Entering her password, she threw her husband under the bus. She'd explain it to him later. "Ian thinks I need conditioning."

A grunt. "Does he now?"

"He's not wrong. Six months in prison and ten pounds of lost weight have made me weak. I'm not much of an exerciser though, and he's so...buff. Virile. He can lift staggering amounts of weight, has freaky roadrunner speed, and, well, you know. SEALs." She rolled her eyes. "I might need you to kill me before four o'clock. He's going to kick my ass, and I'm going to totally embarrass myself. I don't even know what half of those things are."

Rory punched her shoulder playfully. "There's an easy fix, you know."

She glanced over with hope in her eyes. "What?"

"Just say no."

Her shoulders deflated and she focused on the screen again. "Easy for you to say. No offense, but I don't have an easy excuse like you not to show up. I mean, he's right—it's not only my brain that's a wasteland right now. I have no strength, no stamina. I'm a wreck from head to toe."

Rory rolled off toward his desk. "I've seen a helluva lot worse, Doc. Don't beat yourself up."

She let it rest for a while, working on the project he'd given her, getting him coffee, as part of their pact, and occasionally making a production out of reading the list. "What's a leg curl?" she called over her monitor.

His fingers flew over the keyboard and a picture of a muscle-bound guy popped onto her screen.

"Why do I have to do three sets of fifteen reps?" She gave a painful sigh. "Please just kill me now. Not only do I not know what the exercises are, I'll die trying to do them. I'm going to be so embarrassed."

One of those infamous grunts. "You don't seem the type to give a flying fig about what someone thinks of you."

"You're right." She sat up straighter and tossed the paper aside. "Who cares if he's a SEAL and his body alone makes me look like a runt? Who cares that I'm skinny and out of shape? I'll play to his male ego, the helpless damsel in distress who doesn't know the names of the exercises or how to do them."

Silence from Rory's desk.

She sank her head into her hands and made a hiccupping noise that might pass for a sob if she was lucky. "Who am I kidding? He's going to laugh at me! He's going to tease me endlessly about this!"

"Oh, for fuck's sake," she heard him growl. "Are you going to work or sit there and whine the whole time?"

"You don't understand." She shot to her feet and glared across the room at him. "You're a man. Even in that wheelchair, I bet you have women fawning all over you. I've built my reputation on never showing weakness, never letting anyone, not even Ian, see me unsure or uncomfortable." Shaking her head, she shut off the monitor. "Forget it. I'm out of here. I can't focus when I know I have to face him and those stupid weight machines in"—she glanced at her watch. Technically Ian's that she'd stolen—"forty-five minutes."

She got to the elevator, hit the button. The doors slid open and she stepped inside, wiping at a pretend tear. The doors were two inches from closing when he called out, "Wait up."

A heartbeat later, the IT guy was inside with her. "What are you doing?" she asked when he punched the button for the basement.

"I'm going to walk you through each of those exercises so your superior image isn't shot to hell and then you're going to get your ass back in that seat and check those numbers, *capisce?*"

She had to roll her bottom lip in to keep from grinning. He would be able to see it in the mirrored paneling. Squeezing her eyes shut as if holding back her tears, she leaned down and threw her arms around him. "Thank you! I owe you big time."

He peeled her off. "No emotional displays, Greene."

"Right." She straightened and tugged on the hem of her blouse, relieved to be able to stop acting.

In the gym, he did as promised and showed her how to use the equipment. She even coaxed him out of his chair at one point to demonstrate how to use something he called a jacked-up rack. He wasn't stable without his crutches, but he was strong and managed to hobble-walk from that machine to the rowing machine.

Once they'd exhausted the list and both of them were sweating, she went to the locker room and grabbed towels. "I can't thank you enough." After tossing one at him, she hitched her thumb over her shoulder as she ran the freshly washed material over her stubby hair. "Mind if I shoot a few hoops before I go back upstairs?"

He gave her a suspicious glance. "You play?"

"Not exactly." She dropped the towel into a nearby laundry bin. "I discovered a long time ago that I needed a way to decompress between patients. Sinking a ball into a basket kept me focused by using a different part of my brain." She hopped on one foot and pretended to do just that. "Eye-hand coordination, you know?"

"Your form sucks."

"I suppose you can do better?" She purposely eyed the chair. A challenge.

He whirled it in a circle. She'd seen him do that once or twice before. It seemed to help him think, like tapping a pen or rocking back and forth in her chair, did for her. "With my hands tied. Let's see what you got, Doc."

Now she was in trouble. She'd never played nor had she done anything more than pitch wadded up paper into a trash can. She always missed. "Lead the way."

There were only a few other employees working out, some using treadmills or the track. One doing calisthenics.

That man hung upside down from a bar. "Yo, Shady." He grunted as he curled up. He had a faint British accent. "You back at it?"

"Just teaching this newbie how to sink a ball," Rory replied.

"You're the new shrink," the man said, eyeing Vivi upside down. "Parker said you're a ball buster."

She detested the term 'shrink,' but she suddenly liked Parker even more. "And you are?"

He hauled his sweating carcass off the bar and landed smoothly on his feet. "Name's Moe, but I go by Henley, and no, I don't need you poking around in my meatball." He pointed to his head.

"Not much to poke, I imagine," she replied under her breath to Rory, but loud enough that Henley heard.

He chuckled. "There's that ball busting. You'll get along all right here, shrink."

"I want to flip him off," she said, again under her breath, even as she smiled at his smug face.

"He gets that a lot." Rory grabbed a basketball lying outside the court lines, smoothly pushing his chair back to her. "Go for it. He'll consider it a compliment."

She kept the smile and raised her voice, displaying the rude gesture. "Keep calling me that, and you'll see how much of a ball buster I am."

He scrunched his face into mock fear. "Skinny thing like you will blow away in a hard wind."

Typical. "Be careful or I'll teach Parker how to hypnotize you in your sleep. You'll be quacking like a duck before you know it."

He made a finger gun and fired it at her. "I like you." He strolled off to the showers.

Controlling her eye roll, she pivoted to take the ball from Rory. The man had a huge grin on his face. She bounced the ball—at least she knew how to do that. "Shady?"

He rubbed the tops of his thighs, probably didn't even realize he was doing it. "Having been a spy and an assassin, I've been called worse."

"I thought maybe it was a reflection of your basketball skills and he was secretly warning me you play dirty."

"Always." Rory winked. "He's right, you know. You fit in well with the rest of us. We can sure use you if you decide to stay."

It was becoming a broken record. Had Beatrice put them all up to this? "That's up in the air." As was the basketball when she fired it at the net. It missed by a good three feet and hit the concrete wall behind the hoop.

"Jeez." Rory watched her rush after the bouncing ball. "You sure you've played before?"

Keeping her back to him, she hid her smile. "You think you can take me, Shady?"

"Hey, now, respect your elders."

She turned and tossed him the ball. "Show me what you got."

Even in a wheelchair, the man was fast and agile. While she'd seen the game played, she had no skills, and Rory wasn't above taking advantage of her.

"Don't tell Beatrice I was on the court with this wheelchair. I'm supposed to use my other one when I play," he said. "Now, plant your feet like I told you, fingers facing the basket. Control your movement, less is better."

Panting, she bent at the waist and braced herself on her knees. She'd already missed five throws. He'd sworn jump shots were the easiest, and had suggested he knew she was lying about her skills. "Why do you need your other chair?"

"The wheels won't wreck the coating on the floor."

"I can go get it for you."

He gave her a wolfish grin. "Need a break all ready?"

She sure did. "Could you at least stand up and show me your trick?"

The grin faded but the challenge sparkled in his eyes. "I need my crutches, you know that."

"I'll get them."

"You wouldn't be trying to distract me so you can catch your breath, would you?"

She straightened. "Nah, if I wanted to distract you, I'd talk about how nervous I am to have Parker hypnotize me, or how scared I am about Ian putting himself out there as bait." *Thud, thud, thud,* she bounced the ball. "There's a part of me that wants to hide here—Beatrice has made that too easy. I want to forget everything that happened, not take the risk of opening that door again. Stay in this cocoon and pretend I'm needed."

He scrutinized her closely, but she kept her eye on the hoop, continuing to dribble. When he didn't comment, she went on. "This place is like your crutches. It's propped me up, but it's keeping me from doing what I know I need to do—walk on my own."

Silence fell between them as she held the ball and squeezed it tight. She didn't throw it, though, as if she were thinking something through.

Finally, he said, "Sometimes we need crutches before we can walk on our own. It's okay to be scared, to need other people, to put off remembering what it used to be like."

Turning his words over, she secretly agreed. But this wasn't about her. "Not my style," she said. "I have to face things, stand on my own two feet. For me, not knowing what I did is worse than hiding my head in the sand and pretending this plateau is okay. It may be safe, but I've never played it safe. I don't intend to start."

She wanted to stick around and see if her words had any effect on him, but timing was everything. If she tried to hammer home that this was really about him and walking again, he would put up a barrier. That wall every human had when they were pushed to face their fears.

Handing him the ball rather than shooting it, she gave him a sad smile. "Thanks for teaching me more than basketball."

Heading for the elevators, she left him sitting there facing the basketball hoop, as well as his fears about standing on his own two feet again.

FIFTEEN

Someone had taken the bait.

Ian sat in Cal's office, their heads down as Cal walked him through the layout of the Reese house, the upgraded security system, and the hidden compartments where he kept weapons.

"The doctor should stay here," Cal said. "She's a distraction. If someone tries to take you out, which we're hoping they will, you'll be too worried and focused on keeping her safe."

Ian didn't need the team leader to tell him that, but he also knew Vivi. When push came to shove, telling her she couldn't do something was like waving a red cloak in front of an angry bull. "I have a plan."

Regardless of how good the computer geeks employed by NSA or whoever was keeping tabs on her old emails, phone records, and bank account information were, Rory was better. He'd called Ian to his hub earlier and showed him, quite proudly, how he had snagged their interest and they had put even more, nearly invisible, triggers on all of her virtual accounts. They knew someone had been looking at them, scrolling through her emails. He wanted them to, and now, because every computer expert and hacker had a signature, he believed he knew who was watching her accounts and would subsequently use the trail of breadcrumbs he'd left to find Ian.

MonkeyFingers was a legendary black hat who'd disappeared in 2018. Gossip among the hacker community ranged from claims she'd gone underground, was assassinated by the government, or had reinvented herself as somebody else. In reality, she'd avoided the hefty prison sentence she'd been handed after breaking into Homeland databases and planting spyware by loaning her services to NSA for the next ten years.

Rory, on the insistence of Beatrice, had been the one to anonymously alert the head bureaucrats at that time about the breach and how to find MonkeyFingers. He knew everything about her since the CIA had once ordered him to assassinate her back in the day when he performed wet jobs.

The world of hacking was no longer dominated by those under twenty-five anymore. These days, the earliest generations were now middle-aged. MonkeyFingers avoided being killed by Rory, but only because he didn't believe her crimes warranted such extremes. He'd let her get away and took the fallout from his bosses without remorse, claiming she'd outmaneuvered him.

Fat chance that, but she was alive today because of him. When the CIA sent the next assassin, he made sure she'd had no choice but to sign on with NSA. The irony was, she hadn't been the person to plant the spyware that got all of them up in arms—*he* had. But he'd made it appear to have her 'signature.'

If she was the one watching those accounts, it meant NSA—and more specifically Command & Control—was behind all of this, and they didn't play nice.

Cal sat forward. "Let's hear this plan."

Ian didn't like sharing, but this was his boss now. He'd only been here a few months and was still trying to earn his trust, as well as the other SFI employees. Still waiting for them to earn his. He swallowed down his unease. "I have arranged for her to be detained by Beatrice. I know you don't like it, but you're part of that plan. I need you to do me a solid."

"Me?"

"You and Beatrice haven't had your sessions about Sloane with her yet. In order to keep her here, guess what? Beatrice is about to rope you into spilling your guts about the night of Sloane's birth and your feelings regarding what happened."

Cal groaned and threw himself back in his chair. "You've got to be kidding."

"Quite the paradox, isn't it? You get to talk about what went down in your house the last time you were there, while I'll be squatting in it, hoping something similar happens."

"I knew I should sell that place when I had the chance," Cal said with a chuckle. "Guess if this works, it will be worth it."

"I appreciate you letting me use it for this. I can't guarantee it won't get damaged or end up with a few bullet holes. I mean, my strategy is to use stealth and cunning to outwit whoever shows so I can interrogate them, but if I have to go Jason Bourne on their asses..."

"Shit happens." Cal shrugged. "There's nothing of real value left, with the exception of my guns. I've been meaning to clear them out, just haven't gotten around to it yet."

"I bet Vivi has a theory on that." He grinned. "I know it's like walking through hell and back to go to therapy, but she really is good at what she does. You might find it helps you, Beatrice, and your daughter."

Cal rubbed his eyes. Ian wondered how much the man slept. He never let himself rest. Because of the demons chasing him? No wonder Sloane had absorbed the underlying anxiety he and Beatrice constantly wrestled with. Shaking his head, as if shaking off the tiredness, Cal blinked and fought a yawn. "I'm not opposed to therapy—in fact, I know how incredibly important it is for all of us. I've just never been good at discussing the junk in my head. Or my heart."

"You and me both, brother." Ian held out a fist and Cal bumped it. "Imagine if you're married to a psychologist like Vivi. I can never tell when she's analyzing me. I assume always, which makes it hard to let my guard down. Seems like the only time I can get her to turn off that big brain of hers is—" Whoops, better back that train up before he offered too much information and embarrassed them. "Well, you can probably guess."

The wolfish grin that crossed Cal's face said he knew *exactly* what Ian was talking about. "How did a couple guys like us end up with wives who are so damn smart?"

"Pure luck?" They shared a laugh, and Ian rose, giving the blueprints a final scan and snapping a photo with his phone. "Think he or she will try to take me alive?"

"They'll send a team."

"My thought, too. If it were me, I'd send at least four to cover the quadrants and two to breach."

"Our ace is that they don't know you work for me. They'll expect you to be surprised and unprepared."

"The surprise will be on them." He strolled to the door. "I'll scout the place and report in once we're in position."

"Henley, Zeb, and Connor are waiting downstairs. Trace will meet you there as soon as he touches down from his latest mission. He and Connor know the house, so trust them to hold the perimeter. Call me if anything seems off."

"Roger that." He offered a lazy salute. "We *are* lucky, you know."

Cal gave a ghost of a smile. "The luckiest. I'll keep your wife busy, I promise."

That was one less thing he had to worry about. Pretending he hadn't set this up with Cal and B was a whole other story. He'd never been able to deceive her.

In the supply room, which was more like a private armory, he and his counterparts loaded up on what they might need. Comm units, flak vests, night scopes, weapons.

Ian didn't know Zeb or Henley well, and he'd never spoken much to Connor, although the kid lived and breathed SFI. Trusting them to have his back made him twitchy, but the members of this organization ran like a well-oiled machine, living and working together. Each had been in battle many times and lived to tell about it. All of them acted like they were blood family, ready to lay down their lives for the others. They were an elite group that got the job done, and there was a rapport between them, as if they'd been on hundreds of missions together.

"I'm best at scouting," Zeb volunteered, adjusting his vest before throwing a lightweight rain jacket over it. "My eyes are still good, even if my reflexes aren't as sharp as yours and Henley's."

"I'm quick on my feet and good at diversions," Connor offered.

"I'm good at everything," Henley said with a wink.

Zeb and Connor rolled their eyes.

Ian was lead and it was his call. He'd had plenty of experience spearheading teams. "We play to our strengths until we know their weaknesses. Zeb, you take the perimeter and report any movement. I'm obviously the decoy, waiting for them to breach. Connor, you're with me inside. Stay out of sight and cover my back."

Henley checked his automatic and stuck it in a shoulder holster. "And me?"

"You run interference if and when we need it. Trace may not arrive before our guests come calling. If he does, put him in position where he'll be of most use. Also, Cal and a few others will be on standby. Call in reinforcements if we need them."

Henley snugged a black cap on his head. "Are we taking any of them alive?"

They'd gathered into a loose huddle, armed and highly dangerous. Ian nodded. "We should expect four to six assailants. We take their leader, if possible. He'll have the most intel."

"We interrogating there or here?" Henley asked.

He seemed entirely too cheery about the idea, but it was a good question. "If we take out the others quietly and don't draw attention from law enforcement, we can do it there. Otherwise, we chuck him in Hell and haul ass back here."

Henley played with a folding knife he'd taken from a pocket in his cargo pants. "Who's in charge of getting our pig to squeal?"

Interrogation wasn't in Ian's bag of tricks. He leaned toward more Zeb-like expertise—scouting, strategy for takedowns, kidnapping, rescue, hand-to-hand combat. Yet, this was his mission, his ass on the line. He had to do it for him and Vivi. He was the one who knew the questions to ask. "I'll handle it."

Henley closed the blade and pocketed the knife. "Bummer."

They checked their comms with Rory, making certain they were all connected and he could give them a heads-up on any traffic in the area. Ian sent each man a photo of the residence's layout. He pointed on the map where he wanted them stationed once they secured the house.

"Our endgame is simple," he reiterated. "We get the leader, find out who sent him. The others are collateral. I don't want them dead, necessarily, but our safety comes first. In the event we subdue any or all and keep them alive, we can use them to send a message to NSA or whoever's behind this, or to negotiate a deal. In any event, do not take unnecessary risks, cover your asses, and let's carry this out as stealthily as possible so we don't get outsiders involved. Any questions?"

His team shook their heads. He stuck his fist in the center of the group. "This means a lot to me," he told them. "I owe each and every one of you a huge favor."

Fists smacked his and Zeb winked. "You don't owe us jack, Idol. You and the good doc are part of our family now. We volunteered for this and we won't let you down."

"I have a knack for getting people to talk," Henley said, backing toward the door. "Just in case you want help with that interrogation."

"Roger that." Ian struggled to keep the grin off his face. He'd missed being part of a team of brothers. Missed feeling this alive—his wife was safe, he had purpose again. "Let's do this."

Adrenaline pumped through his veins inside Hell as Connor drove them out of the garage. Since he'd rescued Vivi, the vehicle had been repainted to a dull white with a contractor's logo on both sides.

Ian rode shotgun, the others in the rear. As the city filled with high-rises, shopping centers, and freeways melted away to subdivisions, cookie-cutter houses, and green lawns, he took a deep breath. He'd dreamed of having a house and kids, but knew he'd never be happy without the thrill of the next mission in his veins.

Could he have both? His conversation with Vivi had him toying with the idea that they might find a compromise. If they wanted, they *could* have a life outside of espionage and military escapades, but would they find satisfaction in the world of 'normal?'

Cal and Beatrice had tried it. Their house sat empty,

quiet. They lived at SFI and that would continue once the compound was finished and they had living quarters there. Was that the answer? Living and working together with others like you?

Most psychologists would say no. Work should be kept separate from your family life, right? There should be boundaries, you should be able to leave it behind at the end of the day.

But he and those like him never did. Which was where people like Vivi came in, showing them how to be at home no matter where they were and what they did. How to compartmentalize and truly be all they could be.

Lost in this thoughts, he didn't realize they'd arrived at the Reese property until Connor said, "Kincaid, we're here."

Homing in on the coming hours, Ian shoved thoughts about his future with Vivi into one of those encapsulated compartments and nodded. If either of them were to have a future and be able to decide what to do about it, he first needed to pull this off flawlessly.

Once inside the house, he made himself at home, checking in with his counterparts who were in position. Then he followed the instructions Rory had given him for leading MonkeyFingers and her handlers right to him. His fingers pecked at the keyboard and he smiled. "Come and get me, suckers."

His phone rang.

SIXTEEN

Vivi was going to tear his head off and shove it up his—

"Hey, babe."

Her whole body shook with anger. "Don't you dare, 'hey, babe' me. You left without me."

Cal and Beatrice had brought two chairs into her office and plucked them down, Beatrice locking the door behind them. "We're ready for our session," she'd told Vivi with a straight face.

"It's just a scouting run," Ian said now in her ear. His voice was light, unconcerned. "I thought it wise to check out the house and the grounds before we move in and become bait."

He was lying. Had to be. He'd *promised*. "And you didn't want me with you, why?"

"Cal mentioned he was talking to you this afternoon, and his schedule is jam packed. He said something about

Beatrice threatening to cut off his you-know-what if he didn't show up."

The couple, dog at their feet, stared at her from their seats, faces neutral. Yep, they were all lying.

"I'm going to kill you." She hissed at them before pacing to the window, her heart squeezing. "We'll discuss this when you return."

"You sound worried."

"I am worried, you moron! Command & Control will kill you!"

"And cheat you out of it?" He chuckled at his own joke and she mentally vowed again to tear his head off. "It's just a reconnaissance mission. I'll be there before you know it. I saw this Italian place on my way here. Maybe we could have a date tonight?"

Attempting to mollify her. Yeah, not happening. "I see exactly what you're doing and I'm not letting you off the hook, Kincaid."

Then he mentioned what he planned to do to her later in bed and her resolve to kill him swayed slightly. Her toes curled and she felt flush as he went into great detail.

She'd kill him *after* he did all those things.

"Now, don't stress," he purred in her ear. "I swear I will do that and so much more to you, and that means I'm coming back to you as soon as I've thoroughly surveilled this place and created a plan for us to lure our quarry here, okay?"

She chewed her bottom lip, her stomach a mess. "Promise me you'll be here before five."

He paused as if checking his watch. "Six at the latest. I want to check out that restaurant on the way. See if they have decent tortellini. I know how you love that stuff."

Bastard. "Not a minute later or I'm coming after you."

"I love you, Viv."

Gah. That was a low blow. "Get your ass back here and prove it."

"Roger that," he said, all casual and sexy. "All night long, *babe.*"

He disconnected and Vivi clamped down the urge to hurl her phone at the wall. She stared unseeingly at the buildings across the street. He called her babe. He only did that when he wanted to rile her up or distract her.

Done and done.

Whirling on his accomplices who were still trying to look innocent and failing, she marched to her desk.

Maggie's ears perked and she whined. Cal went on high alert, or at least higher than his normal hyper-vigilance. He automatically reached for Beatrice's hand and she took it. They both looked terrified.

Good. Vivi caught herself before she said things she might regret later. She was angry at all of them, but mostly herself. Ian had crawled under her skin again, made her care too much. If she lost him now, after everything...

Clenching her jaw and forcing herself to breathe through her panic, she resumed her seat and met Cal's hard gaze. "One hair. One eyelash. So much as a *hangnail.* Anything happens to him, I will walk out of here and wash my hands of you both. Are we clear? Then I will sneak back and kill you in your sleep."

"And leave Sloane an orphan?" Beatrice squeaked.

"She has a family here, doesn't she?"

Beatrice looked chagrined, but Cal said, "I can't guarantee nothing will ever happen to Kincaid. He's a soldier; it's in his blood. Wrapping him in a cocoon serves no purpose, and there is risk involved in each and every action we take. You know that." Beatrice squeezed his hand, attempting to make him shut up. He didn't. "He's skilled, trained, and can handle whatever happens. You can't protect him from the world."

He held her stare a heartbeat longer, then slouched in his chair. Beatrice closed her eyes and made a face, seeming to brace herself for Vivi's reply.

She considered chucking her desk lamp at Cal. Getting up and walking out. Yelling obscenities and more threats.

None of those things would ensure Ian's safety. Cal, damn him, was correct—the world was not a safe place. Ian could fall in the shower, be involved in a car accident, have a heart attack. All unlikely, but things like that happened each and every day and she couldn't cover him in bubble wrap, no matter how badly she wanted to.

From her drawer she selected a pencil and snapped it in half. The splintering noise caused Beatrice to jump slightly and her eyes flew open. Maggie shifted, uneasy.

That accomplishment did little to ease Vivi's anxiety but the physical act of doing *something* took the edge off her anger. Inside her mind palace, she catalogued the sensations coursing through her, then shoved them into a box. Dropping the individual pieces into her empty waste can, she forced herself to breathe again and detach from the betrayal she felt over what had happened.

She slid on a pair of readers and cleared her throat, her

therapist persona saving her from drowning. "We've covered the details of the events that transpired the night of Sloane's birth. What I want to review is how you felt about it."

Both glanced at her as if she'd grown six heads. Keeping her personal stuff separate from everything else made her feel like she had.

Beatrice released Cal's hand and fiddled with the hem of her blouse. "Some moments, it was frightening, but we handled it."

Handled. The term was often used in place of 'controlled.' Control was an illusion. "You had no control over the woman invading your house during the event. I assume you had a birth plan, and having your life and that of Cal and Sloane's threatened wasn't part of it."

"Of course not."

It was challenging to get folks like the two in front of her to examine their gut-level reactions to threats, but Vivi had found using certain language helped. "We've discussed how you responded to the physical threat, and handled the attack with your quick-thinking and bravery. What reactions did you experience internally when the event arose?"

Blank stares were the answer. Were they reliving it in their minds or refusing to open that door?

Vivi put herself in their place. "Normal people would report fear, anger, panic, and perhaps also the push of courage, justice, and retribution. Do any of those terms describe how you felt while it was happening?"

Cal relaxed a smidge, tapping his thumb on the armrest and nodding. "All of them."

Now they were getting somewhere. "Protecting your family put your skills and training to good use, correct?"

Another nod.

"But the idea of losing them may have also caused extreme fear. That fear, when not expressed and released, builds. It causes flashbacks to events you experienced while in the field. Nightmares. Like a bullet wound leaves a physical scar, the trauma of the event leaves emotional and mental ones."

"We're aware of that." Beatrice shifted and crossed her legs. "How does that affect Sloane? What happened happened. We can't go back and change it."

Vivi made a note. "I think we can."

"How?" Cal asked.

"Reprogramming her memories. Creating a whole different scenario for her. Has she asked about her birth? Seemed curious?" Children often did, and Sloane seemed very attached to her dolls. She'd explained to Vivi how each had been born during one of their play sessions.

Beatrice shrugged. "Once or twice, maybe."

Vivi flipped the pages of her notebook and ran through her bullet list. "We're going to use a multi-pronged approach, recreating and acting out a much more gentle and safe scenario for her, reinforcing it with stories about her birth that would be considered normal. Nothing upsetting. I've already downloaded a track of sounds in the womb and she and I listened it to it this morning. We discussed what it was like to be a fetus inside your mother."

"How will that help?" Cal asked.

"When brain cells fire at the same time, they wire

together. Through sound and story, we're going to get new ones to fire and wire in a different way. We're also going to use Maggie and..." She glanced at her notes. Sloane had one friend, a younger girl who belonged to Jon and Jaya Wolfe. "Neptune Star, to model safe, relaxing sleep. I'd like you to contact her parents and fly her in to stay a few days."

The couple glanced at each other. "Anything else?" Cal asked, as if she were a kid with a Christmas list.

"Sloane is too young to hypnotize and the virtual reality units might cause more anxiety, so we'll start with these simple, basic exercises. The two of you will write out a happy, peaceful story about her birth and memorize it, telling it to her on a regular basis. While her hand-eye coordination is still poor, she's demonstrated a love of coloring and I can coach her to recreate her birth visually, once she's heard the tale from you a few times. This will embed it more deeply into her subconscious. She may also find it easier to use drawings or toys to express trapped emotions she's working through over the real event. I'll need to see her daily for a while."

Cal stood and clapped his hands, rubbing them together. He was obviously anxious to leave. "Sounds good. We done here?"

Vivi kept the evil grin off her face, forced her eyes to remain impassive. There was so much more she planned to do to him. "Sit back down, Reese. Your time isn't up yet, and we have a lot to discuss about your PTSD."

He tensed. Maggie licked his hand. "I really need to run."

She pointed at the seat with her pen. Beatrice grabbed

his hand and gave a tug. "It can wait. Let's hear what she has to say."

Vivi bit the inside of her bottom lip. *Gotcha.* "Let's start with when Rory, who was still performing wet jobs for the CIA, came after Beatrice."

Cal dropped into the chair and glared at her. Maggie laid her head in his lap. "You can't be serious."

She was going to break him like she had that pencil. "How did you feel when your wife was being tracked by an assassin? When she came to you for help? You were in the middle of a divorce, correct?"

"How do you even know about that?"

Beatrice sighed loud enough to echo in the room. "You've been talking to Rory, haven't you?"

"The two of you have experienced more trauma between you than most go through in an entire lifetime. You're surrounded by a bunch of folks you call family who are also carrying heavy loads when it comes to what they've encountered and lived through. This isn't only about helping Sloane sleep better, it's about creating a home life, no matter how abnormal, that isn't also dysfunctional as she grows. Hiding her away from the world because there is actual danger is one thing." She pinned her focus on Cal. "You accuse me of wanting to place my husband in bubble wrap, and claim it won't work, but that's exactly what you've been doing with your daughter. What will happen when she's old enough for school? When she wants to join the soccer team? Go for ice cream with friends? Date?"

The terrified look returned. He eased back in his chair, as if creating distance from her could buffer her statement.

Maggie rose and leaned against his legs. "She's never dating."

Beatrice hid her smile. "We've learned to take things one day at a time. We'll figure all that out when it happens."

Vivi shook her head. "That's a nice, safe plan. For now. That girl comes from strong, intelligent, and courageous stock. She's surrounded by people who take chances and risks every day. You better confront your fears about her growing up now, because she isn't going to be a wallflower. She's going to challenge you at every turn, and you can build all the compounds you want to hide her in—it won't work."

They both reared back, the accusation hitting them like a physical blow. Beatrice's eyes were hard, her voice low when she spoke. "That's not why we're building the new headquarters."

"Isn't it?" Vivi challenged.

Maggie whined and pawed Cal's knee. He petted her and stood, pulling Beatrice with him. "We're done here. Thank you for your time, doctor."

He'd be back. Despite his and Beatrice's reaction, they'd come around and realize Vivi had hit the nail on the head. More than once. She pounded it into the ground. "I expect your written version of a peaceful birth on my desk before noon tomorrow, and fly in Neptune for the weekend. I'll see Sloane in an hour. Any questions?"

Cal blinked, a deer in headlights. "Are you always such a hardass?"

Vivi stood, closing her notebook. "Yep, just like you with your teams. If you want us to succeed in stabilizing your daughter's mental and emotional well-being, step up and do the work."

He grunted, leading Beatrice to the door. "Keep the chairs," he said as he ushered her through. "You'll need them."

He might have been psychic, or knowing him, had prearranged her next visitor, who stuck her head in as they were leaving. "Got a minute?" Dr. Thorpe asked, her face bright. "It's about Rory."

Reining in her 'hardass' self, Vivi pasted on a smile and motioned for the woman to enter. "Everything all right?"

"Better than," Amelia said, sitting on the edge of the chair Cal had just vacated. "He's resuming his therapy tomorrow."

"That's great news."

Her smile faltered. "It is, but..."

"But what?"

She grimaced. "I have a quandary."

Of course she did. *I'm going to kill you, Cal Reese.* This had to be his doing to continue keeping her busy while Ian was gone.

What could she do about it? She'd already decided she wasn't going to live in fear, yet today, that stupid emotion had tugged her around like a dog on a leash.

She'd just given Cal and Beatrice a lecture—one she had to turn on herself as well. *Ian is fine.* He knew what he was doing. It was only a scouting expedition.

Vivi opened her notebook to a fresh page and adjusted her glasses. "Why don't you start at the beginning?"

Twenty minutes later, she'd helped the physical therapist understand that her attraction to her patient was healthy and normal and not unethical. Vivi had advised her to talk to Beatrice if she felt her feelings for Rory overshadowed her work, but assured her Beatrice was thrilled that she'd given him a new lease on life.

Afterwards, Vivi picked up her cell and saw there were no texts from Ian. She typed a message, deleted it, tried another. Then she set the phone down before sending it.

She was obsessing again, stuck in a fear state, rather than a confident one. Putting her notebook away, she locked up her desk and was about to head to her room when Parker arrived.

"I hear you want to train me to hypnotize you." The woman offered a friendly smile. "Moe told me you'd have me turn him into a chicken."

Blaming Cal and Beatrice for these constant interruptions was tempting, but Amelia definitely hadn't been recruited to search her out and discuss Rory. Maybe Parker was here on her own accord, too. "He seems like a handful."

She loitered in the doorway, eyeing the new green wall. "Do you offer couples counseling?"

The day's events had exhausted her, especially her worry over Ian. Leaning on the edge of her desk, she rubbed the back of her neck. "You and he...?"

"Yep, and we're a hot mess. He throws up a lot of walls because of his childhood. Likes to piss people off and typically runs on sarcasm. I know it's all subconscious, but I want more. I want him to trust me and open up to me."

"He'll never come to counseling."

"Is that your professional opinion?"

Sure was. "I know the type. You're in for a long haul."

"Would you be willing to give me some ideas for breaking down his walls?"

"You want to see me as a patient?"

She nodded. "I could really use someone to talk to."

Vivi stifled her sigh. What would it hurt? "I'm no expert on love, but we can explore a few ideas. Reverse psychology comes to mind."

Parker grinned and then glanced over her shoulder, as if making sure he wasn't eavesdropping. "I've had training in hypnosis, by the way. I had access to your training videos when I was head of Project 24."

"Training videos?"

"The ones you made to demonstrate the results of Trident." Parker seemed slightly abash. "C&C wanted me to try similar things on the soldiers in the program."

"Those assholes." She shook her head. "Those videos weren't meant for that purpose."

"I wish we'd known each other back then," Parker said.

"What exactly do you do here?"

"I'm head of the spy division."

Vivi nodded. "Impressive."

"We're having a team meeting next week to go over some new protocols. I'd like to introduce them to you and Trident. I think they could all use an outlet for their work."

"You are sucking me into staying here, whether I want to or not."

Parker grinned. "I believe one of the reasons Trident is so effective is your compassion. Most of us in the field try to have it, but we're very focused on outcomes. On solutions. We lose some of our empathy along the way. Patients sense that. You make people feel better just by talking."

Vivi thought it over. "I give them hope. That's what's missing from many therapies."

"I could use a refresher with the hypnosis, but any time you want to give it a try, I'm game."

Vivi brightened. That would make things easier. Quicker results, she hoped, too, if she didn't need to spend weeks instructing Parker and having her practice. "And you haven't already compelled Henley to do your bidding?"

They shared a laugh. "I've been tempted, believe me," Parker said, "but he's too strong of a personality. Do you think it can unlock your memories?"

"Only one way to find out, right?"

Holding up a finger, Parker glanced over her shoulder again. "Beatrice asked me to bring you a gift. May I?"

Curious, Vivi nodded and pushed off the desk, straining to see what the woman was backtracking to grab. Her breath caught when a large bird cage, covered with a colorful cloth appeared in front of Parker as she entered once more.

Vivi nearly fell to her knees. "Are those my...?"

Parker grinned. "Took a bit to track them down but they're healthy and happy. Where do you want me to put them?"

Vivi cleared a spot on her desk and slowly removed the material covering the cage. Inside, two sets of dark eyes peered back at her. "Hello, my sweet friends," she murmured.

Parker peered at the tiny birds. "Parakeets, right?"

Vivi fought back happy tears. "Also known as budgies. They're quite social and friendly."

"What are their names?"

"Sherlock and Watson, although Ian always called them Batman and Robin."

Sherlock perked up, cocking his head and whistling a greeting. Watson hopped up and down on his perch. "Ian," the bird squawked. "Lord of the Wings!"

Parker laughed. "They can talk?"

Vivi nodded. "Watson often does, and Ian has obviously taught him a few phrases. They were in a rescue after their owner died. I thought I wanted a cat." She'd been at a low point in her life then. "Instead I walked out with a bonded pair of budgies."

"Cool," Parker said, poking a finger in and wiggling it at them. "A bird doesn't seem like an affectionate pet. What do you do with them?"

Sherlock loved to sing. Watson liked to sit on her shoulder. He often rubbed his head against hers in a display of affection. They'd both brought her so much joy. "That's just it—they're low maintenance and you simply let them be birds. They require some exercise, but in general, they're beautiful and loving and even good with kids."

"Can we let them out?"

She definitely owed Beatrice a huge favor for tracking them down. "Close the door and we will."

It took a bit of coaxing, but she managed to get them to

venture out onto the desk. They took flight, swooping around with delight. Eventually, Watson landed on the top of the desk and moseyed over. Vivi gently petted his head.

"GenGen," he said in his bird voice.

"Dr. Gen was what a lot of my patients called me," she told Parker, "since my first name is—*was*—Genevieve."

Parker held out a finger for the bird to examine. "You need a Rock Star codename now."

"Why? I won't be in the field. Won't be here much longer."

Parker met her gaze. "I'm sorry to hear that. You have such great compatibility with everyone."

"Codename." Watson hopped onto Vivi's shoulder. "Anchor word. Come to me, little bird."

The room spun. Her stomach lurched. She sagged against the desk, the edges of her peripheral vision filling with dark spots.

"Vivi?" Parker's concerned voice sounded far away. "Dr. Greene?"

Inside her mind palace, Vivi heard another voice. "*Sherlock*," it had taunted that day over the phone. "*Come to me, or your husband will be tried and executed in front of the entire world.*"

The image of Ian outside that hotel flashed through her mind. Her last thought as she slid to the floor while Parker yelled for help, was, *save Ian.*

SEVENTEEN

Sixty minutes passed, then ninety. Not a blip on their radar, no moves in fact at all by the one they wanted.

It took time to put a team together, sure, but had their quarry decided to stand down?

Ian paced the living room, the kitchen, the dining area. He'd double- and triple-checked to make sure he'd followed Rory's instructions to the letter. He'd definitely let those watching know he was hunting the truth about Genevieve Montgomery's actions on that night and how he'd been redirected from his original mission to kidnap Alon and instead had supposedly killed her.

He fingered his mic. "Coldplay, this is Idol. Any movement? Over."

"Zip," Hunter responded. "With the exception of the family a click to the west returning home fifteen minutes ago, it's been me and the birds. Over."

"Roger that." His frustration continued to build. "Sit report. Anyone else?"

All replies were negative.

Birds. He thought of Vivi and her precious budgies. How much she loved those damn things.

She might have left him behind, but those little guys? Never.

How many times had he gone over it in his mind? It didn't add up. Her leaving her cushy office. Getting on a plane and flying to Berlin.

Speaking of... He checked his phone but there were no messages from her. He definitely owed Cal a steak dinner and six-pack. Whatever he was doing to keep her busy seemed to be working.

But if nobody showed soon, he had to call it quits, at least for tonight. Hunter had joined them half an hour ago, the others holding their positions and staying silent, all of them waiting for any sign that their enemy was on the hunt.

So far, crickets. Rory had confirmed that nothing of interest had come across the sites he monitored, and there was no sign that MonkeyFingers had viewed Ian's online searches or tampered with any of the intel he was searching for.

It was as if those monitoring the information had suddenly and thoroughly disappeared.

Typical of NSA or Homeland. But were they the only ones keeping tabs on a dead woman?

He wasn't sure where that left him. Where it left Vivi. If their government, who'd been so provoked by the Jim

Lawrence incident that they'd denied one of their premier psychologists a fair trial, threw her in a black site prison, had cared enough to keep tabs on her accounts and files until now, what had caused them to drop it in the past few days?

If it wasn't an alphabet branch, then who? Lawrence himself? The man was no cyber genius, but had he added one to his ranks?

Had he wanted to add Vivi to his network, too? Get her under his control in order to hack her mind palace, as she always referred to it, and gain the ultimate intelligence on the U.S.?

A crawling sensation on the back of his neck had him staring at his cell and considering his next move. Return to SFI and take the abuse she was sure to heap on him? Remain put and see if anyone eventually joined them?

His team wouldn't care if he decided to stay, but explaining it to her would cause a backlash he didn't want. He wasn't ready to quit just yet, though, and Cal had to be running out of ways to keep her distracted.

His phone buzzed in his hand, and he grimaced at the ID—Beatrice. She no doubt wanted an update and might be the person to force him to wrap this mission up for tonight. "Yeah," he said, bracing himself for her to pull the plug. "This is Idol."

"Return to base. We have a problem."

His instincts went Code Red, the crawling sensation spreading to his chest. "What?"

"Our favorite detective has experienced a setback. I can't say more." Her voice lowered, even though their phones were encrypted. "She needs you."

He white-knuckled the device. While they hadn't said

it to her face, they'd nicknamed Vivi "Sherlock." Not a rock star name, but a fitting one nonetheless. "Is she okay?"

"She's under surveillance. Won't talk to anyone. I'm hoping you can get through to her."

Holy shit. Had she remembered something? "I'll be right there."

HIS CRAMPING STOMACH fell to his knees when he saw her in the hospital bed. Her eyes were closed, lines running from various parts of her to the machine hooked up at her side. His stomach fell to his feet when he saw the handcuffs around her wrists, securing her to the rail.

He stormed into the room. "What the hell?"

Dr. Sloan glanced up, closing the chart he was reading and meeting him halfway across the floor, placing a hand on his chest to stop him. "She's going to be okay," Jax assured him in a quiet voice. "Those are only for her own safety. We should talk outside."

He needed to touch her. To let her know he was there. "Get out of my way."

Jax stared him down for a heartbeat before shifting aside. "She needs rest. I'll fill you in outside."

Ian walked past him, striding to the bed and taking her thin hand in his. It was cool and dry, lifeless. The cuff clanked against the metal side rail.

He leaned over and placed a hand on the side of her head. "I'm here. Everything is going to be fine."

Jax cleared his throat from the doorway, and when

Vivi didn't respond to his voice, Ian swallowed hard and reluctantly left the room.

Jax wasn't one to beat around the bush. "Her vitals are strong and she seems healthy by all accounts, but I believe she's suffered some type of mental break. Her bird apparently said something right before she experienced a panic attack, then blacked out. When she came to, she tried to leave the premises and was acting completely out of it. Distant, not speaking, like something was compelling her to leave, and she had no control over herself. I had to sedate her."

Ian blinked, processing it all. "Her *bird?*"

Jax nodded and explained what had transpired, how Beatrice had tracked down the pets and Parker had brought them to her right before the episode occurred. "I know this sounds bizarre, but I suspect Vivi has had someone use her own hypnotherapy on her."

Ian ran a hand over his face. "How is that even possible? She told me you can't be hypnotized unless you want to be."

"That's true, in general. I'm not sure who or how someone could use it on her, but her reaction suggests they have, indeed, planted a trigger word or phrase in her mind that causes her to act unlike herself. When I asked her where she was going, all she would say was to save you."

"Holy fuck." His stomach cramped so hard, he nearly had to bend over. "Is it possible that's what caused her to walk into Lawrence's compound that night?"

"I suspect so. Until I figure out what the hell is going on, and break whatever this spell is she's under, we have to keep her contained here for her own safety. I was hoping that if she saw you, it might end the control of the hypnotic state."

"Then what are we waiting for? Wake her up."

Jax looked him over. "Take off all that gear first. If she sees you wearing a flak vest and armed to the teeth, it won't assure her you're not in danger."

Right. "Give me three minutes."

He discovered Beatrice waiting at his doorstep when he arrived at his room. "I knew there was something fishy about her not remembering what happened," she said at the same time he asked, "How could she have been hypnotized?"

They stared at each other for a moment. "She's too smart to let anyone manipulate her," he insisted.

"Intelligence isn't the determining factor. Neither is willpower. Did she ever mention Command & Control to you?"

"No." That crawling sensation returned. "What's that?"

"A directorate inside NSA that's part of the President's threat matrix team. It doesn't officially exist because it's *the* top secret branch of the NSA. When I joined that directorate, that's where I met Genevieve. At that time, there were only six members, and we were all under immense pressure. They brought her in to counsel us. She was bright, ambitious, and she proved herself loyal. They sent her to the CIA Farm in order to undergo training so she would have an understanding of what undercover operatives experienced in the field. When she demonstrated that she could handle that kind of pressure herself, they offered to send her on assignments. She turned them down, but ended up becoming a therapist for a select group of spies as well—those whose missions involved assassination. More patients with unhealthy amounts of pressure on them. Her methods were so successful, they opened up her services for men in Special Ops."

He hadn't known the details, but he'd figured as much. "And?"

"The President gets a daily hitlist—people who are direct threats to him, others in high ranking positions, the country. Those in C&C decide who gets taken out and how—it's often made to appear a suicide, an accident, or an inside job. We're talking leaders of other countries who might be looking the other way when it comes to threats against us. CEOs of billion dollar companies who might be financing terrorist activities. Important people in the public spotlight."

He was following, yet not. "What does this have to do with her?"

"She knows the truth behind many of those *accidents* because the assassins who performed them went to her for methods to manage their conscience afterward."

His mind shot off rapid-fire theories. "Lawrence, or whoever orchestrated this, wasn't after intel on undercover operatives, he wanted the dirt on our government's illegal activity. The chancellor?"

A dip of her chin. "Most likely. Someone planted a trigger to get her to willingly give up that information once they could blackmail her, using you."

"Nobody showed up tonight because they don't care if I look into her death. They're simply keeping tabs on anyone who sniffs around her accounts."

"They may still target you if they get the slightest whiff you're a whistle blower." She sighed heavily and pinned her gaze on the wall as she continued to speculate. "Our government needed her contained that night because she was indeed a threat to national security. We have to get the evidence to show that it wasn't her fault. Even then, they may not be willing to look the other way. She's under some type of neurological programming, and finding the person responsible is the only way we can prove it."

"How?"

"There are few who know about Command & Control. I'm asking you to keep this to yourself so you don't make Vivi even more vulnerable, but I don't see how Lawrence could have the ability, training, or opportunity to embed a trigger in her head."

"You think this top secret NSA directorate is behind it?"

"Yes. Trace and Parker have both had dealings with them, and they believe the same."

"Back to my earlier question—how do we prove it?"

"They used you to get to her, to make her believe that she had to save you. When did you become her patient?"

He nodded. "After a failed mission. Our unit lost a man. We were all handling it in various, unhealthy ways. I never underwent her Trident therapy, though."

"Was it your CO who ordered you to receive counseling?"

"The directive came through him. No way he's involved." Cuswell wouldn't have anything to do with it. "It has to be someone else."

"Came through him from whom?"

He shrugged. "No idea. I got the order to show up and I went. Begrudgingly, but I did."

"Were any of the other men ordered to see her after the failed mission?"

He went still inside. "No." It had bugged him for weeks, but he'd been infatuated with Vivi and let it go. "Only me."

"Were you already sweet on her?"

Sweet on her. Such an old-fashioned phrase. "I'd seen her around, heard about her treatment. A friend with such bad PTSD he had to withdraw from the program went to her. She helped him a lot with Trident. Yeah, I wasn't cool with seeing a therapist, but since it was her, I figured I'd get to know her. Maybe ask her out."

"You married in Vegas. Did anything odd happen while you were there?"

"Odd how?"

"Any accidents, even insignificant ones, like someone bumping into her or shoving her? Strangers seeming overly friendly? Did Vivi feel ill? Act out of character? Anything at all."

"We stayed at a rental and went out for a late breakfast the morning after. A waitress spilled coffee on me and I went to the restroom to try and get the worst of it off my shirt. When I came back, Vivi seemed kind of out of it. She said she was fine, but..."

"Any chance you noticed security cameras around the place?"

"We purposely chose one that didn't have any. I mean,

we were trying to keep our marriage under wraps until I was able to complete my final mission."

"Which turned out to be rescuing her."

"We're chasing our tails with this."

"Maybe not. What was the name of the restaurant?"

"Kaleidoscope. It's a dive in the burbs."

"I'll need the information about the rental."

"Fine, but I need to get back to her. See if she remembers anything."

"I want a detailed list of everywhere you went, anyone you spoke to, anything else you can think of that seemed off at any point from the time your CO sent you to her for counseling until that night at Lawrence's."

"What about Jack Spear? Could he be behind this?"

"At this point, I'm not ruling out anyone. I doubt that's his real name, so I've got Rory digging."

Frustration roared through him. He punched the wall, leaving a hole in it.

"I should take that out of your next paycheck," she said with a teasing note in her voice, "but I won't. I understand your anger, and I feel the same. What we have to focus on is getting her to snap out of whatever this is. Then we'll learn who did this to her and make sure they pay."

They were going to pay all right. He gritted his teeth. "They put her through hell. Me, as well. When we get them, I'll handle it."

She planted her feet, a blockade. "I'm all for justice, but we are not vigilantes, and if you go against C&C, you are likely to disappear and end up six feet under in the desert. That won't help her. You're part of my team, part of Shadow Force, and we have ways of dealing with entities like this without getting the whole group in trouble. We will avenge what happened to Vivi, but we do it smart. We find the evidence and make sure it's handed over to the right people. I've done this kind of operation before. We don't go off half-cocked."

In the back of his mind, he knew she was right. Justice had always been an important pillar of his life. Revenge was not.

Problem was, he'd never had somebody close to him targeted. This was personal. "I won't make promises I can't keep. I'll do things your way when and if I can, but if the situation presents itself, I will kill whoever did this without hesitation."

Her displeasure was obvious, yet she stepped sideways, allowing him entrance to his room. "I'll hold you to that. Just so you know, if you defy my orders, I will make your life miserable, and you'll be promptly dismissed from SFI."

He nodded, reaching for the doorknob. "Understood."

Inside, he shed his gear, stripping down to his T-shirt and replacing his cargo pants with plain jeans. The T-shirt Vivi had worn last night was casually tossed on the nearby chair. He picked it up, holding it to his nose and breathing in her scent.

Someone had taken his wife, with her big heart and even bigger brain, and turned her into a weapon.

Oh yes, he would make them pay.

EIGHTEEN

Vivi woke feeling like she'd been drugged. Her head swam, her vision blurred, and her mouth felt stuffed with cotton.

She *had* been drugged, as evidenced by the tubes running from a vein in her arm up to an IV pole. Lifting her hand, she went to rub her eyes...

Metal clanged against metal. Her arm stopped in mid-air and she jerked it again. *Clang.*

What the hell?

Blinking, her vision cleared enough for her to see the cuff on her wrist. Even though it was pointless, she jerked it a few more times, frustration building.

Ditto for her other hand. She was handcuffed to a hospital bed, with no memory of how she'd gotten here or why. "Hello?" she called. "Someone get me out of these cuffs!"

As if she'd conjured him, Ian burst through the door

and rushed to the bedside. "You're awake. How do you feel?"

She sat up, causing the room to spin, and promptly fell back onto the pillow. "What happened? Why am I chained to the bed?"

He gripped her hand. "We think you've been hypnotized, possibly had Trident turned on you. Do you remember being in your office with the birds?"

Her temples throbbed. "My birds?" She shook her head, then stopped when pain shot down the back of her neck. "I haven't seen them since the day I flew to Berlin." None of this made sense. "What do you mean I've had Trident used on me?"

As she lay there feeling helpless, he told her what Beatrice suspected. What he suspected. Her stomach cramped, her mind seeming to slam every door in her mind palace as she tried to make sense of what he was saying.

"It's not possible," she argued. "I couldn't have been hypnotized, with or without my permission. I would know."

That was an error in her thinking and they both knew it. Obviously, if she had been, the person doing the manipulation would fabricate it so she didn't remember.

Ian squeezed her hand, and brushed a strand of hair from her face. "We have to consider the possibility. It would explain things, the inconsistencies in your behavior in Berlin."

Fear raced through her system. Just the thought of it made her shiver. For anybody to have done this, she would've had to have trusted them, let them into her circle, which was exceptionally small. She didn't trust many people, and for someone to have betrayed her like this...

She couldn't wrap her damaged mind—or her heart—around it. "There has to be another explanation. My brain is just broken."

The crease in Ian's forehead deepened. "The hell it is. Come on, Vivi, think. What would Sherlock do?"

His voice held a challenge, yet kindness as well. He understood how difficult this was for her. "He would keep searching for the truth."

"Exactly." He glanced back at the open door. "Doc! We need these cuffs off."

Dr. Sloan appeared before he'd finished. He tossed the key to Ian. "Vivi, how are you feeling?"

Ian undid the heavy restraints. With him supporting her, she managed to sit up without the world going lopsided. She rubbed her wrists. "Like crap. Did you sedate me?"

He looked sheepish. "Had to. You were acting like a zombie and tried to walk out of HQ."

Speechless, all she could do was stare. Jax checked her blood pressure and listened to her heart. The argument against their claims continued in her head, but she felt hollowed out.

Find the answer, she heard her father say. *There's always a solution.*

There had to be one key missing piece, if only she could remember it. Everything would fall into place if she could.

Ian laid a hand on her leg as Jax finished, interrupting her thoughts. She shut her eyes for a second, trying to recall her birds and what had happened before she'd attempted to walk out of SFI. There was just...nothingness. A blank.

Precisely like the day she'd flown to Berlin and boldly marched into Lawrence's compound.

Her stomach pitched and she was floundering for something, *anything,* to vomit into. Ian, as always, had some acute sense that alerted him right before she shoved Jax aside and managed to upchuck in a small waste can he flung up to catch it. It was such a violent retching, she had to grab the railing and hang on, but then it was over and Ian was holding her head and saying soothing things as he encouraged her to lie back.

"Would you like some anti-nausea medication?" Jax asked.

"No." Her voice was a croak, her throat raw. She waved a hand in the general direction of the door. "No medications. Just rest."

"Of course." The doctor gave Ian a knowing look over her head that she pretended not to see. "Beatrice is taking care of your birds, so don't worry about them."

She desperately wanted to see them, but if they were part of this, if someone had used them to get to her... She held in a curse. "Beatrice has enough on her hands. Ask Parker to do it."

"Will do." Jax put a steadying hand on her shoulder. "Don't stress. We'll take care of you."

After he left, she motioned for Ian to close the door. Easing herself up, she took a deep breath and waited for him to return.

"I know that look," he said, sitting next to her. "What are you thinking?"

"Someone used me and turned me into a traitor," she hissed. "They used Sherlock and Watson to control me."

"I know." He took her hand again. "Do you remember the day after we married, when we went to that cafe? Kaleidoscope?"

What did that have to do with anything? "What about it?"

"When I went to the restroom to wash the coffee off my shirt, what happened?"

She shrugged, once again feeling confused. "I sipped mine and waited for you to come back."

"Did anyone approach you? Speak to you?"

"Why are you asking about that morning?"

" Could that be when you were hypnotized?"

"In public during the few minutes you were in the restroom?" She shook her head. "I don't remember anything odd, and that's not a likely scenario. To put me under and plant a trigger in my subconscious would take a highly trained expert over a period of time, working on my subconscious without my knowledge. It couldn't have happened that morning, and it has to be someone I trust deeply, whom I would never suspect."

"Who fits that description?"

Her head pounded, her mind unwilling to go there. To think about the few close friends she'd had, and the fact one had betrayed her. Violated her. "Get my notebook, would you?"

"How about you get dressed, and we'll retrieve it together?"

He didn't want to let her out of his sight. She couldn't blame him. "Hand me my clothes."

UNSTEADY ON HER FEET, she had to lean on him as they walked. The weakness made her angry all over again.

Who had done this to her? More importantly, how was she going to track them down and reveal their complex scheme to the world?

Whatever it took, she had to do it. She had to clear her name, banish the shadows from Ian's face. Give the two of them a fighting chance for a future.

At her office, she pulled up short. Her ears rang and her vision darkened, as if she were about to pass out. *Save Ian.* "Wait," she choked. "Make sure the birds aren't in there."

He cracked open the door and then gave her the all-clear. "Are you okay?"

She swallowed the lump in her throat. It was fear, plain and simple. A fresh wave of anger rolled through her, and she grabbed onto it like a lifesaver, accepting her husband's supportive hand. "I'll be fine. My notebook should be in my desk."

No sooner had he got her seated then Beatrice appeared in the doorway. Rory, on crutches with his leather bag, followed.

"I hear our patient is up and about," Beatrice said, looking Vivi over. "Have you remembered something?"

"Only that I wanted to save Ian." She leafed through the pages of her notebook. "I'm sure that was the trigger, not a specific word that Watson said." All eyes were on her as she tried to push past the pain throbbing between her temples and find a logical explanation. "A bird is an unreliable tool to activate any type of subconscious programming. Think about it. Sure, mine can mimic human speech, but they tend to speak words randomly." As if her brain had received a cue, a stray recollection of her and Parker discussing the birds flitted across her mind. "Codename," she murmured.

"What about it?" Ian asked. "Is that the trigger?"

She shook her head. "No." She held up a finger, trying not to lose the thread from earlier. "Give me a second."

GenGen

You need a Rock Star codename.

The cache in her head began to spit things out. The cage, Watson hopping up and down, Parker's wiggling finger.

Those in her office stared intently. Pieces of the puzzle danced around each other, a bottomless sensation in her stomach.

"I believe my reaction earlier had more to do with my fear that Ian was going to be ambushed on that jaunt he went on. Something about that scared me and made me recall the message and picture I received that day with a threat. That's what triggered it."

Ian sat on the desk. "The photo of me in front of that hotel?"

She nodded. "The day is still a blur, but I remember now that it showed up in my email with no explanation, then a copy of it was on my desk, again with no explanation." More images flooded back to her. "I didn't know what to do with it. Why someone kept showing it to me."

She shook her head as if that could clear the void.

"What does *codename* have to do with it?" Beatrice asked.

"I used codenames with patients when I logged them into my calendar. It was a layer of security that made them more receptive to opening up about things."

"Regardless of privacy measures surrounding our employment," Ian explained, "those of us who live under the gun and use false identities to keep our real ones secret felt more at ease knowing our name wasn't splashed all over her appointment book."

"I used names of animals, like eagle, hawk, cobra, and the likes, along with my own personal coding system."

"How did you keep track of all that?" Rory asked.

She tapped her temple. "My memory is typically very good. Every patient I saw has a separate room inside my mind palace that contains facts about them and what we discussed during their sessions." Giving her head a harder tap, she shut her eyes and tried to remember why the term codename had caused her to blackout. Why she'd felt over-whelmed with panic.

Push through. Find the solution.

Inside her palace, she heard a phone ringing. "I received a call right before I left that day. The person on the other end told me to come to him or he would..." A hot lance seared up the back of her head and into the spot between her eyebrows. Grabbing the edges of the furni-ture, her breath caught. Her mind was fighting back.

There was that goddamn wall she had to get past. "I can't... It's too..."

Ian swiveled her chair around and bent down in front of her, grabbing her wrists. "You *can* do it. Look at me, Vivi. Remember."

Tears burned her eyes, but she blinked them open. The cool green of his irises met hers. She blinked away the tears and drew another shaky breath. He was her rock. He wouldn't let them hurt her again.

More importantly, he *was* safe. Safe here at this place, surrounded by these people. *Family.*

It's what the two of them had dreamed of.

Gritting her teeth, she stared into his undaunted eyes and shoved on that mental wall. *I can and will remember. Ian is safe and so am I.*

"Deep breath," he commanded. Always the soldier. The leader. Her warrior. "There's no hurry. I'm not going anywhere. I love you, and nothing that happened that day will change that."

"*He's all you have,*" the voice had taunted, "*and I'll take him from you, too.*"

Something snapped inside her, fear morphing into rage. She felt the wall give.

As if it were as fragile as Sherlock and Watson's wings, the memory of those words fluttered on the outskirts of her mind. Breathing like Ian instructed, she forced herself to relax and reel them in.

Come to me, little bird...

Save Ian...

Her eyes flew open as the words repeated.

"I remember!" The sentences felt trapped, though.

"He said..." She swallowed, cleared the lump in her throat, and tried again. "*Come to me, little bird, or your husband will be tried and executed in front of the entire world. He's all you have, and if you don't do as instructed, I'll take him from you, too.*"

Expecting him to be upset at the threat, she was surprised when Ian smiled. Still, the commander in him issued another directive. "Good. What else?"

Beatrice and Rory exchanged a glance. She squeezed her eyes shut, recalling the rest. "He told me to get on a plane and gave me the address for Lawrence's compound. Told me I was expected. *Save Ian.* That's the last thing I remember him saying."

Beatrice stepped to the desk. "Did you recognize the voice?"

Vivi opened her eyes. "No, he disguised it."

Rory sat in the visitor chair, laying his crutches on the floor. The bag rested in his lap. "That suggests that you *do* know him, and he was covering his tracks." He withdrew a sheet of paper, sliding it to her. "I recovered your calendar and printed off the list of patients you saw that day. The codename thing makes sense of these seemingly random terms. Cobra Red 12, Phoenix Snicker Monster."

Ian released her hand and looked over her shoulder as she swiveled to glance at the names. "You really do have skills," she said to the computer guru. In the back of her mind, she was glad he was using his crutches again. "Cobra Red 12 was a female CIA operative who always wore red lipstick and considered 12 her lucky number. Phoenix was an analyst who survived a fire as a kid and loved snickerdoodle cookies." At their semi-confused looks, she said, "Cookie Monster?"

Ian snorted. "Your brain is...well, weird, but somehow it works."

"At least it used to," she grumbled.

He rubbed her tight shoulders. "What was your code-name for me?"

"Teddy Green," she said. "You continually brought me gummy bears and your green eyes have always relaxed me."

He chuckled and kissed the top of her head.

Beatrice moved to her other side and scanned the codenames. "Our perpetrator may be on this list. He had to get close to leave that photo. Do you remember your sessions with any of these patients? Could one of them have planted it?"

Ian pointed at a name in the margin. "Dr. Crowe? Who's that?"

Vivi's breath caught, her world turning upside down. *Find the answer.*

She just had.

NINETEEN

Ian knew the second everything fell into place for her.

"No one," she said. "I was supposed to call him is all."

Beatrice eyed her closely but his wife didn't so much as blink. "Who is he?"

"My therapist." Vivi gave a short laugh that sounded forced. "Even I need help sometimes. Once a quarter I was required to check in with him. He'd been sanctioned by Homeland, although he wasn't employed by them. He was—probably still is—a consultant. I would discuss anything bothering me and go through a check system about my health and stress levels. I was overdue so I made a note to contact him."

"There's no one else that raises a red flag?" Ian asked, taking the spotlight off this Dr. Crowe. He'd get to the truth of it as soon as Beatrice and Rory left.

She studied the codenames again. "Afraid not."

"Vivi." Beatrice returned to the other side. "What about the trip to Vegas? More than one of my employees has had, shall we say, unfortunate outcomes when visiting there. Ian mentioned you experienced an incident at a cafe."

She sat back in the leather chair and rubbed her forehead. "That was nothing more than a morning-after freak out. Ian and I had put our careers on the line when we wed. Our original plan was to not take vows until he'd finished his last deployment and his term was up. My resignation was going to be harder to negotiate, but I had a back door that I felt was solid. I'd already signed every confidentiality statement they threw at me, but I was willing to do whatever NSA, Homeland, the President, you name it, required in order to make a clean break from my duties and assure everyone I would never become a threat to our country. I mean, I married a SEAL. Can't get a better bodyguard than that, right?"

Ian winked when she glanced at him.

She toyed with the pen. "I had a written agreement outlined with my plan to create a new identity and check in with Homeland on a regular basis to ensure I was sticking to it." Her gaze dropped to her desk, but he knew she was seeing the future they'd talked about. "Others had done it successfully. I was going to do it, too. For us."

Her pretty eyes met his once more. All the hardship they'd endured in the past six months, all the self-loathing he'd stored inside him, believing he'd killed her, the trauma she'd gone through, dissolved in that gaze.

I will fix this. He would make it right. "You need rest. How about we get you back to your room?"

"Before you do," Beatrice said, "I want the names—the real identities—of everyone on that list."

"That would be a breach of doctor-patient confidentiality, but under the circumstances, I'll share. I know you won't let their names fall into the wrong hands." She clicked the pen and began writing. "Again, I'm certain none of these people were involved."

When she finished, she slid the paper to Rory. He placed it inside his bag. "And your mentor? You're sure about him?"

She spread her hands wide in a supplicating gesture. "He's a professor, an outsider to all of this. Impeccable background, of course, or they wouldn't have let me see him. He never knew the specifics of my job, and I wouldn't have shared them. I would've put him in danger if I had. He treated my father, another brilliant soul who was completely off his rocker in his later years. I trust Dr. Crowe."

Rory gathered his crutches and stood, Beatrice walking him to the door and opening it for him. "If you think of anything else that can help us..."

Vivi nodded and yawned. "I'll let you know."

Once they were gone, Ian gathered her into his arms and held her for a long moment. "You didn't fool any of us, you know."

She drew back, meeting his eyes and giving him a grin. "Didn't I?"

That's when he knew he'd been had. Beatrice and Rory, too. "It's *not* Dr. Crowe?"

Breaking his embrace, she gathered her notebook and pen. At least she'd stopped rubbing her head as if it were about to explode. In fact, in the last few minutes she'd completely morphed into the confident woman he'd fallen in love with. "Oh, it is, but not in the way you guys suspect."

"Are you going to fill me in?"

"On the way."

He trailed her out the door. Thunder rumbled in the distance. "Where are we going?"

She paused at the elevators, glancing around to be sure Beatrice and Rory were gone. Lowering her voice, she leaned in as she pushed the bottom button. "Can you get us out of here without them knowing?"

A challenge to be sure, but when had he ever backed down from one? "What are you up to?"

"I got myself into this mess, and I'm going to get myself out. We are dealing with highly sensitive information and people who won't think twice about obliterating all of us if they realize I'm alive and still walking around. Our government believes I'm a traitor; proving I'm not is possibly the most difficult thing I've ever done, but if I play my cards right, I'll be free. *You'll* be free. And there won't be any blowback on Beatrice or SFI. Will you help me?"

The elevator dinged and the doors slid open as he stared at his version of Sherlock Holmes. She was more like Irene Adler, the woman Holmes was obsessed with. "Did you just bat your lashes at me?"

She grinned cheekily. "Did it work? Are you wooed by my feminine wiles?"

Of course he was. He escorted her inside, then backed her against the wall. Smiling down into her eyes, he ran his hands up her sides. "If I remember correctly, I took a vow that I would be there for you, no matter what, for better or for worse."

She trailed her fingers through his hair, her gaze landing on his lips. "Fair warning, things *could* get a lot worse."

"Or a lot better." He dropped a kiss on her mouth. "I don't fucking care. As long as I'm with you, I'll go through hell and back. Ten times. A hundred, if that's what's necessary to make you happy."

She pushed up onto her toes and kissed him. "I love you, Ian."

"I suppose you're going to have to start calling me Teddy Greene."

"Not if I do this right. If we have to go on the run, though? I hope you're good with it." They shared a laugh and another kiss. "You're distracting me," she said as the elevator opened on their floor.

"Is it working?" he mimicked, batting his lashes at her. "Are you wooed by my masculine wiles?"

She playfully smacked his arm. The storm hit with force, rain slashing against the window at the end of the hall. He followed her to her room, enjoying the extra strut she put into the swing of her hips.

"Don't ever stop flirting with me," she demanded. "No matter how old we get, or how comfortable in our married life, promise?"

"Promise."

Once inside, he shut and locked the door and made good on cherishing her one last time before he snuck her out of SFI headquarters and into the dark, stormy night.

. . .

"MY FATHER WAS AN ACCOMPLISHED PHYSICIST, but his superior brain had trouble with any type of normalcy. My mother did her best to cater to his mood swings and mind periods, but it was tough on their marriage."

Ian glanced across the seats to where she sat as the SUV cut through night, the headlights reflecting off sheets of rain that poured over them. Visibility was terrible as they took a country road into Virginia. She'd never opened up about her family before. "Mind periods?"

She chuckled. "That's what mom called them. It was like a version of PMS, where Dad's mind would go into overdrive and he would lock himself in his study. The walls were covered with chalkboard paint so that he could scribble formulas and mathematical equations in streams around the room. The periods would last for about a week, and it was all she could do to get him to eat or sleep. It always caused adverse effects, and afterwards he would practically be comatose for days. It was like his brain would download something and he had to vomit it all out. Then he had to recover. It happened approximately every thirty days or so, and that was another reason Mom termed it a period."

"Dr. Crowe helped him?"

"His real name is Dr. Ardy Lippenstein and he used hypnotherapy on Dad." She scratched at her short hair. He knew she missed her long locks. He did, as well. They would come back, just like her memory. "Dad had gone to many doctors and experts, all of whom put him on drugs. Those only seemed to exacerbate the problem or turned him into a zombie. His health began to deteriorate faster and faster. Hypnosis unlocked a different part of his brain that helped him moderate the outbursts. It was truly amazing, and probably extended his life by several years."

"I had no idea it could do such a thing."

"It was quite experimental and revolutionary, and Dad became fascinated with psychology. Even considered trying neurotherapy. He taught me a lot of what he learned, and I became intrigued with the brain and its functions, too."

"So Crowe is another codename?"

He heard the smile in her voice. "I loved Bruce Willis' character in *The Sixth Sense*, Dr. Crowe. Hence, I used it for Lippenstein."

"And you started going to him as a patient when?"

"I was a teenager when Dad began seeing him, and sometimes I drove him to the sessions. Since I knew I wanted to go into psychotherapy, I was fascinated with Dr. Ardy's techniques and asked him to let me sit in on some of them. Dad was cool with it, and at home, we would practice on each other. When I went to college, he and I kept in touch, and he helped me demonstrate my technique for my Ph.D. Eventually, I ended up at NSA and in need of my own therapist. I called him."

The SUV's navigation instructed him to turn right in a hundred feet. "How does this tie into what happened? You haven't explained that yet."

An oncoming car's headlights spotlighted her for a brief moment. "As we discussed, manipulating me would take someone highly trained. Someone I trusted, and it wouldn't be a person easily flagged by my employer."

He was going to kill the guy. "Dr. Lippenstein."

Her gaze swung to him and he caught her smile out of the corner of his eye. It was full of cunning. "Yes and no. He had a part in it, I believe. What I'm unsure of is if it was intentional or not."

"I assume you're going to let me in on what you're thinking at some point before we actually confront the man."

She leaned over and patted his thigh. "I hope you're good at playing things by ear."

"I prefer to have a working game plan."

She slid her hand higher and he sucked in a breath as her fingers grazed his cock. "I know, but I don't actually have one yet."

He groaned, both from her confession and from her 'evil feminine wiles.' "What if this guy *is* the man behind all of this? What if he uses some trigger word and causes you to go off the deep end again?"

Her fingers gripped him through his pants. "That's why I brought you. You're going to protect me, in case he tries anything."

His words came out strangled. "Now the truth comes out."

She chuckled, releasing him before she pinched his leg. "You big, bad SEALs are good for something."

"*Former* SEAL."

An assessing pause. "Are you sorry you left the brotherhood?"

Was he? Some days, if he were being honest, yes. He missed the hell out of it. Others, not so much. "I do, but SFI has filled that hole for me. Sort of." He glanced over at her. "If we work this out, I'm happy to leave them, though."

She nodded. "I get it. Maybe you won't have to. The group—*family*—has grown on me. It wouldn't hurt us to stay for a while."

The navigation instructed him to take the next drive. "Are you sure he still lives here?"

"The estate has been in his family since the Civil War. Plus, Rory just texted me his address." She gave a rueful chuckle. "He's still here."

"Told you that you didn't fool anyone, but damn, I disabled every tracking device this vehicle has, plus our phones. I thought for sure I'd gotten us out without that bastard knowing."

"He's as good as he claims."

He drove past the mansion looming on their right. "So are you." He pulled to the curb a block down, near a fenced pasture. "Since you don't have a plan, I do."

"Care to share?"

Slipping the SUV into park, he cut the lights and shifted to face her. "First, it involves you staying put until I secure the premises. He may be under watch by our government friends, or have significant security in place. I don't want to tip any of them off that we're here."

Her head was outlined by a flash of lightning in the distance. "Logical. Then what?"

He grabbed the bag of weapons he'd stolen from SFI and handed her a stun baton. "I promise to come back for you. After all, you're the one who's wired and knows the right questions to ask." He'd made sure they could record the doctor's confession, or whatever information he might volunteer. Next, he handed her a comm unit and walked her through syncing it with his and demonstrating how to use it. "I want your word that you'll let me motivate him if he needs it. My, shall we say, incentives, may not be to your liking, but we don't have time to string this out. We need facts, evidence, a confession, *something* to resolve this as quickly as possible."

She gave a heavy sigh, not liking what he was suggesting. He knew it took all her faith in him to say the next words. "You're the expert."

A huge step for her, giving her consent to harm someone. He didn't care for the idea either, but at times, it was called for. "I won't kill him, even if I pretend otherwise. We need him alive."

This seemed to relieve her mind and she gave him a grateful half smile. "Roger that."

He made her test the earbud again, hoping to reassure her that he was in reach, even if he wasn't physically close. "Keep the doors locked and stay out of sight until I'm back. Do not engage with anyone who isn't me."

He started to bail, the bag of goodies in tow, when she grabbed his arm and yanked him back. "You're the one who needs to stay alive, you hear me? Be safe."

He dropped another quick kiss on her lips. "Always. I'll be back."

"Maybe I should have given you a different codename. Terminator," she called after him with a laugh.

He shut the door, shook his head, and slunk off for the mansion.

TWENTY

Vivi worried her bottom lip and then glanced at her cell. Where was he? How long did it take to check for Big Brother?

Fiddling with the stun baton, she started to raise him on the comm, needing to hear his voice, but stopped herself. Fear was driving her again and she wouldn't let it. *Courage.*

Ian knew what he was doing. He was methodical and an expert at stealth. If anything bad had happened, she would know, thanks to the earbud.

Still, she worried.

Her phone buzzed. A text from Rory. *Is he home?*

She was under Ian's orders not to engage with anyone, but her fingers itched to reply. Beatrice and Rory knew they had defied orders and snuck off the premises to do just this. She owed her friends an apology, but she had to do this on her own.

She clicked off the message without responding.

Please forgive me.

Rory, of course, was undaunted. *If you don't tell me what the hell is going on, I'm sending out a full team to hunt you down.*

Oh boy, she certainly didn't want that. She considered different replies, settled on: *No need. Everything is under control.*

She prayed it was.

No one came or went on this rural road, and she was grateful for that. While she waited for Ian, and wondered if Rory would try again, she surveyed the area. A horse barn with an outside light shone in the distance through the storm. At least the rain was moving off.

She tapped her fingers against the phone. Where was Ian?

Seconds ticked by. Again, she considered touching the earbud and saying something to him. Asking if he was all right. Her knee bobbed. She almost engaged Rory just for a distraction.

And then her door swung open and she gasped, a shadowed face looming over her.

Instinctively, she swung her weapon and a swift hand caught the barrel before it made contact. "I see your reflexes are still good," Ian drawled.

Adrenaline coursed through her and she huffed a curse. "You scared the daylights out of me. A little warning might have been nice."

"Sorry." He took her by the arm and drew her into the lingering drizzle. "The exterior looks clear, outside of a normal security set up. Easy to bypass. But there could be bugs and hidden cameras inside.

"There aren't," came a gruff male voice through their comms.

"What the fuck, Rory," Ian said, glancing skyward as if the man were God. "How did you find us?"

"You clearly underestimate me." They heard clicking on his keyboard and Vivi felt a sinking sensation in her already uptight stomach. It was her fault, she knew it. He'd tracked them via her reply text. Damn it. Rory was gruff. "He's in the study on the main floor watching *The Bachelor.*"

"What?" She'd never expected that. Pouring over *Psychology Today* or writing notes on patients, sure, but a reality TV show? "You're kidding."

"Are you wired?" Rory asked.

"I am." She slid up the hood of her jacket. "Listen, I appreciate what you're trying to do for us, but—"

"Shut up and get in there. Get this over with. I have an engagement tonight."

Her hackles rose, but then she considered his statement. "Something involving a certain physical therapist?"

"What?" He snorted. "PT isn't until tomorrow."

Oh. She screwed up her mouth and sighed.

"We're going in," Ian said. Now who was gruff? He'd probably figured out Vivi had somehow led Rory right to them. "Comms silent."

"What's your plan?" Rory asked.

Ian growled, "None of your damn business. We're handling this."

Rory didn't seem the type to let it go, but he did. "Roger that, Idol."

The comm went dead. "Let's go," Ian murmured to

her and they took off, not down the wet street but through the field and into the back yard of the mansion.

He moved like a shadow and Vivi wondered if she should have her eyes checked when this was over. Even with him close enough to touch, she had trouble seeing him, he blended in so well with the surroundings.

After they avoided the cameras and crouched at a cellar door that creaked slightly and set her teeth on edge when Ian lifted it, they both froze. He rooted around in his bag of toys to pull out a can of WD40. Like duct tape, he'd always claimed it worked on everything. Two quick blasts of the lubricant on the hinges and it lifted with a silence she couldn't believe.

He was good at this. Great at it, in fact. Part of her was proud. Another quite shocked that he'd brought her on such a potentially perilous mission.

On feet as silent as a cat's paws, they took the stone steps into the basement, him guiding her so her wet soles didn't slip. Pitch black closed in around her, the only illumination coming from the entrance behind them, feeble in its ability to light the space beyond the first few steps.

The place stank of mildew and rot. She tried to keep her mind from drumming up childhood fears of snakes, rats, and giant spiderwebs.

While those were easily tamed, the one where a deadly assassin lay in wait to kill them was not. Her pulse spiked, heart hammering in her ears. The image of the prison they'd put her in engulfed her. No rats or spiderwebs, but a similar crawling sensation swept through her bones, as if she were confined once more.

Her mind flashed to her birds. She was never sticking them in a closed cage again.

Her fingers trembled as she reached to grab onto Ian. She couldn't make out his form in the darkness, couldn't tell where to place her next footstep.

Her hand fell through open space. Where was he?

She tried again frantically. Touched nothing.

"*Ian,*" she whispered on a shaky breath.

A hand caught hers when she waved it in front of her. "I'm right here," he told her softly.

She took a breath and pushed down the panic. When had she become such a wuss? He'd questioned her courage; now she was.

Compartmentalize!

"Grab on," he said, shifting her hold to his coat and forcing her to grasp it.

Hanging onto him, she noticed he moved slowly, deliberately, finally flicking on a small flashlight.

The beam showed decades of old furniture, dilapidated storage boxes, shelves of forgotten tools, and miscellaneous items. There were plenty of spiderwebs, too, and a few insects that ran here or there, or were already dead, feet in the air.

Oh, so carefully, Ian took the wooden stairs leading to the first floor. He tried each, noticing which creaked or groaned before trying a different section or completely stepping over them. She mimicked his every move.

Her phone buzzed before Ian opened the door at the top. "Phones off," he whispered urgently.

Dumb, dumb, dumb. Of course she should have done

that. She removed it to do so and saw Rory had sent another text, this one with an attachment.

Hurriedly, she opened it, then held the house's floor plan up for Ian to see. He scanned the photo and nodded, then made a slashing motion across his neck. She wasn't sure if that meant he was going to kill Rory or he wanted her to kill the phone. Either way, she set the device to silent.

On they went, avoiding the study. The jingle of a commercial echoed faintly over the hardwood floors and up to the high ceilings.

Ian led her past antique tables and outdated furniture, positioning her in a nook off the front entryway. He pressed his lips close to her ear. "When I give you the signal," he whispered, "I want you to rattle the doorknob and kick over the coat rack loud enough to get his attention. Once he's out of the study, I'll sneak in there and wait for him to return. Don't let him see you until I call you in, got it?"

She nodded. *Roger that.*

When his voice came over the earbud a few minutes later, her pulse had spiked again and she found it hard to control her breathing.

But she did as instructed, rattling the big old brass knob as hard as she could and sending the tall, wooden rack, with a raincoat and umbrella still dripping from a recent outing, crashing to the floor.

For good measure, she picked up an oriental vase from the nearby side table and hurled it across the entryway. The additional act may have been unnecessary, but damn, it felt good.

TWENTY-ONE

"Go," he'd said to Vivi over the comm. Hidden in the shadows near the study, he felt his blood pumping in his veins the way it had the night he and Ranger had rescued her. Never in a million years would he have believed he would have brought her on a mission. But, here they were. "Engage distraction."

He anticipated the metallic noise from the knob and the clatter of the coat tree hitting the floor. What he hadn't expected was the sound of breaking glass.

His fine-tuned ears made him cock his head. Not glass —china. His mind instantly locked on the large vase he'd seen in the entryway—had his wife smashed it?

Regardless, it got the job done. The doctor, in his robe and slippers and half-asleep, jerked up and came to his feet. "What was that?" He stuck his head out before emerging fully from the room. "Hello?" Lippenstein called.

When only silence followed, he toddled into the hallway, still on alert. He carried an iron fire poker as a weapon. As soon as he was clear of the entrance, Ian slipped inside.

And waited, hearing the man grumble and complain, double-check the door lock, and call out, "Who's there?"

Maybe the old guy would chalk it up to ghosts. Ian prayed he, himself, didn't run into any. A place this old had to be full of them.

While it seemed an unreasonable fear for a guy like him, it was one of the few things in life that freaked him out. His foster mom had always watched ghost hunting shows and grisly horror movies, forcing him to join her when his foster father was at work. Those memories still gave him nightmares.

As he expected, the doctor began inspecting the various rooms to make sure he was still alone and there was no intruder. When he disappeared up to the second floor, Ian tapped his earbud. "Study," he told Vivi.

She slipped in a moment later, grinning from ear to ear. Ian flipped off the television, throwing the room into a shadowed gloom. A single banker's lamp on the desk gave a soft glow.

He guided her to the long curtains framing a window and made her step behind the thick, velvety fabric. "Stay here until I give you the signal. And don't go off script. Please."

That grin was hard to beat. "It felt so good to smash that vase! I think I need more destruction therapy in my life."

"Hold that thought." He patted her shoulder. "Weapon ready?"

She held up the baton. "Ready."

Once he had her in place, he pulled out the fancy ergonomic chair at the desk and sat, placing his Glock on the blotter. He couldn't wait to see the look on the man's face when he returned.

The minutes dragged on. Vivi became impatient. "What's he doing?" she whispered loudly. "Did he go to bed?"

That was a possibility, but Ian doubted it. The unexplained destruction in his entryway should keep him awake and on edge for a while. They simply needed to bide their time until he returned. The element of surprise was crucial. "Patience, Grasshopper."

She huffed. "Afraid I'm running low on that."

Ian heard the creak of floorboards. "Ready, player one."

"What does that mean?" She sounded panicky.

"He's coming. Hold tight."

The doctor bombed into the room, the poker still in his beefy hand. His head was partially bald, and he wore glasses. Initially, he didn't notice Ian sitting there, but seemed more concerned that the television was off. "What in the world," he muttered, going to his recliner where the remote sat on the arm and grabbing it.

Ian cleared his throat. Clearly startled, the man yelped, fumbled the remote, and dropped the poker. "Have a seat, Doc. We need to talk."

Lippenstein froze, sheer terror on his face. "Who are you?"

Ian fingered the gun. "Doesn't matter. Tell me what you know about Dr. Genevieve Montgomery."

The man's flabby jaws went slack. "Gen? What about her?"

"Explain your involvement in the events that happened before her death."

He straightened, bushy brows scrunching together. "I have no idea what you're talking about. Get out of my house. I don't care which agency you work for, this is a clear violation of my rights, and I demand you leave."

"Not until you answer me."

He started to say something, stopped. His lips thinned. "I know about Command & Control. That's who sent you, isn't it?"

Interesting. "Why would you assume that?"

"You're denying it?" The man nodded as if confirming his theory to himself. "I don't know why Genevieve turned traitor. I've already told everyone that. Whatever she was planning, she didn't confide to me about it."

There was no obvious tell that he was lying. "She wasn't a traitor. Someone used hypnosis to manipulate her. I think it was you."

"What?" Disbelief colored his face. As if the wind had been knocked out of him, he sunk into his recliner. "It can't be."

"Why not?"

"She's far too smart to let it." He was vehement. "I've known her since she was a girl. Like her father, she had one of the most brilliant minds I've encountered. She used her intelligence to help other people, like I've tried to do. Until, that is, she turned on us."

Ian rocked slowly in the chair, as if he had all night to sit there and chat. "You considered her your equal?"

A bit of fire had Lippenstein straighten again. "Intellectually, she was superior to me. I don't like to speak ill of the dead, but she had limitations."

Ian tensed, half expecting Vivi to burst from her hiding place and demand he explain that little bomb. When she didn't, he relaxed slightly. "Like what?"

"Well, obviously, she thought herself above the law."

"Prior to her defection, what limitations did she have?"

"Why are you asking me this? She's dead. What does it matter?"

Ian stopped and leaned forward, lowering his voice and injecting steel into it. "It matters because someone betrayed her. Regardless of what you think, I know for a fact she was controlled by someone else. If it wasn't you, then you better help me figure out who it was, because I'm not leaving until I do."

The man blustered, fidgeting with the sleeve of his robe. "You can threaten me all you want, but it wasn't me. If Command & Control doesn't know who it was, I'm sure I don't."

"He's lying." Vivi stepped from behind the curtain, no longer able to restrain herself. "I can hear it in the cadence of his voice."

The man's shock had him scooting back in his chair. "Genevieve?"

He nearly tipped the recliner over when she flicked on the stun baton and raised it to his chest. "They blackmailed you, didn't they? They wanted to know how to control me, so they came to you. There are only three of us who knew my trigger—you, me, and Dad. He's dead. That leaves you."

Ian had to give her credit for her dramatic entrance. The man couldn't seem to form words, couldn't wrap his mind around the fact he was staring at a—yep, Ian had to say it, at least mentally—*ghost*.

"I..." He pressed into the chair again. "How is it you're...?"

"Alive?" She moved the stunner closer to his chest. "I may have limitations," she said with a sneer, "but I'm one hard bitch to kill."

His gaze fell to the weapon, Adam's apple bobbing. "I had nothing to do with it. I would never manipulate you."

She leaned forward and waved the weapon in his face. "Do you know how I know you're lying? It was the way you phrased the threat. You said, 'He's all you have, and if you don't do as instructed, I'll take him from you, *too*.'"

His Adam apple bobbed again. "What...what are you talking about? How does that implicate me in this?"

"One word. One common, every day word. *Too*."

The saggy jowls quivered. "That's not a hypnotic trigger word."

"It refers to Dad. Losing him sent me into a panic for months. You're the only one who knew that. You treated me. You figured losing Ian, the man I loved, *too*, would affect me the same way. Potentially breaking me. My mind."

"Your deduction has flaws."

"Does it?"

"I have no idea who Ian is."

She was smart enough not to take her eyes off the man, simply flicking a thumb over her shoulder. "I didn't have a chance to officially introduce you. Dr. Lippenstein, meet my husband."

Ian gave the guy a lazy salute.

"He's a trained killer," Vivi went on. "He gets testy when people set up his wife and then lie to her. So, doctor." She stepped away and rested her hip on the edge of the desk. "You better start talking."

"I..." Clearly he was at a loss for words yet again. "You." He peered at Ian. "I've seen you before."

"We've never met," Ian told him.

The man shifted to the edge of his seat. "You came to my office several months ago. I remember now. You said you were one of Genevieve's patients. That she had referred you."

Vivi shot him a look. Ian shook his head. "The only therapist I've ever been to is her."

"The photo." Vivi set down the weapon. "That makes twice you've been impersonated. Jack Spear?"

Ian frowned. "A long shot, but seems possible."

She pinned Lippenstein with a glare. "You saw him as a patient, the man who looks like Ian? What kind of help did he want?"

"His name was...Terry. Alan Terry. He told me he'd washed out of The Farm. That he didn't know what to do. It was his dream to work for the CIA. You wouldn't treat him because he wasn't an operative, so you sent him to me."

"*I* sent him to you?"

"Beatrice said Spear was an alias. How many sessions did you have with him?" Ian asked. "Did he come here to the house?"

"I saw him at my office in town. He was depressed and had no purpose, so I put him on anti-depressants and started behavioral therapy. He only came twice, then disappeared."

"You never mentioned him to me," Vivi said.

Lippenstein shrugged. "I planned to ask you about him at our next appointment. I was concerned about his depression, but then you..." He rolled his hand a couple times. "You know."

Vivi paced in front of the desk. "How did he find out about my dad? How could he possibly have planted a trigger in my brain that made me follow his instructions?"

The doctor shrugged. "He said that you'd told him about you and your father's game of hypnotizing each other. That you thought I should use a similar technique with him and your preferred trigger word."

She stopped mid-stride, aghast. "And you just told him what it was? Without checking with me?"

"He had the recording."

Ian felt his blood run cold. He shot to his feet. "What recording?"

"The one you did at MIT," the man said to Vivi, "demonstrating your technique."

Vivi swallowed visibly. "What?"

"He claimed you'd given it to him so I'd know what you thought would work best for him." He stared at her, realizing the mistake he'd made by trusting the man. "Oh, Genevieve, I'm so sorry."

Ian's wife clutched her stomach and leaned on the desk for support.

Ian got the gist of it, but was unclear about the details. "What does that video demonstrate?"

She lifted her pretty eyes, now filled with dismay. "How to control me. Dad and I took turns, demonstrating how it worked. I utilized the video as part of my thesis. Whoever this imposter is, he must have gained access to it."

He wanted to ask what the word was, but didn't want to activate it. "How do we switch it off?"

Lippenstein came to his slippered feet. "I'll do it." He faced Vivi. "I'll put you under and remove it."

Ian wanted to tell the man to sit his ass down. He certainly didn't trust him to use any type of mind control on her.

But she was already nodding, inhaling sharply, and straightening once more. "Now," she said, her voice tight. She set the baton down. "Get it out, *now.*"

Lippenstein motioned her to his recliner.

As she practically fell into it, Ian rose and picked up his gun. "Vivi, are you sure this a good idea?"

The doctor gave him an indignant glare. "I know what I'm doing. I'm the only one who can, in fact, put her under."

"He's the only one I've trusted, besides my dad," she explained.

Ian still didn't like it. As the therapist grabbed his desk chair and slid it across the floor toward her, Ian stepped to his side. The man sat and Ian pointed the gun at his temple. "One wrong move and you're a dead man. You do anything other than deactivate this command—"

"I know, I know." Lippenstein waved a hand at him.

"I'm dead. You've made yourself clear. Now let me get to work, young man."

Vivi gave him a weak smile and he watched helplessly as the therapist put his wife into a hypnotic state.

It took several minutes of guided relaxation, and while Ian was keyed, he realized he felt more focused simply listening to the doctor. He watched Vivi's chest rise and fall slowly and rhythmically.

Which is why his neck prickled when he sensed another presence in the house.

Two steps toward the study door and he tapped his comm. "Rory, tell me you've got someone nearby."

"Hunter and his team are on the way," came the reply. "What's going on?"

"We've got company."

The man appeared, filling the doorway. Dressed in a pale summer suit, he smiled with menace. "We finally meet," he said, "and you brought Genevieve with you. I've been searching all over for her."

Ian was looking at the spitting image of himself. He trained his gun on the smug face. "Who the fuck are you?"

A low, vicious chuckle. "Come to me, my little bird," he said. "Time for us to go."

To Ian's horror, Vivi came to her feet.

TWENTY-TWO

I an fired at the man but he'd already ducked back into the dark hallway. "Wake her up," he ordered the psychotherapist. "Now!"

"Genevieve," Lippenstein walked with her as she passed the television and headed for the doorway, seemingly oblivious of Ian. "I'm going to make a noise with my fingers and you'll wake—"

A gunshot rang out and the doctor went down, blood blooming from his stomach and staining his robe.

Idiot! He'd taken his eyes off the open door to stare at his wife.

"Idol," Rory said in his ear. "What the fuck just happened? Report!"

"Make one wrong move," the man in the hall called, "and I'll shoot her next."

Ian grabbed Vivi's arm. She stopped but stared at the space in front of her. "Vivi, wake up." He snapped his fingers in her face, mimicking what he assumed Lippenstein was about to attempt and hoping that would do the trick.

"Come to me, my little bird," the man crooned. "Don't let anyone stop you."

She started walking. Ian grabbed her and jerked her out of the line of fire. "A unit of highly trained SEALs are about to descend on this house," he shouted at the bastard. "Get out before they fill you with lead, Spear. Or Alan, or whoever the hell you are."

There was a pause, as if he were surprised Ian knew his various identities.

"That's right," Ian grunted around the knee Vivi jammed toward his groin. He was too quick and she missed, but he'd probably have a bruised thigh come morning. "I know who you are. Know you washed out of The Farm because you couldn't cut it." He needed to keep the bastard focused on him. Use what he knew to unsettle the guy, trip him up. "You may be smart, but you're still a fucking grade-A failure."

Another pregnant pause, brief but telling. "A failure?" His voice was silky, yet forced. "I've managed to get a genius psychologist whose head is filled with highly classified information to follow my every order." The bastard chuckled. "I've been working on this plan since the first time I saw her at The Farm. That's where I met her. So talented. Pretty, too. When they cut me, I knew how to get back at them, at everyone, and your wife was the perfect way to do that. I've kept track of her for years."

Ian felt sick to his stomach. Vivi tried to knock the gun from his hand, refocusing his attention. He had to holster the weapon to keep from accidentally shooting her. Her hand-to-hand combat, as evidenced by the fight she was currently putting up, was a problem.

He tried to grab hold of her wrists without injuring her. "So you were jealous," he jeered. He managed to snag her fist when she swung at his cheek, but then she made to bite him. "You couldn't run with the big dogs, so you looked for a pawn to play off against them."

"I found my skills and intelligence were appreciated by others."

"Jim Lawrence?"

"To the highest bidder go the spoils. He paid handsomely. The United States had it coming, and I'm just getting started. Once I get that bitch back to Jimbo and he scrapes every last bit of intel out of her, my reward will be enough that I'll never have to work again. I'll be on the beach with a rum in each hand, a whole new man. She'll be on her knees, begging for mercy."

Ian saw red. He prayed Hunter and the others were closing in. Subduing Vivi *and* fighting his alter ego simultaneously was definitely unexpected. Beatrice had been right—every mission held the ability to blindside you. Vivi had managed to do it now three times.

And two of the three, he'd handled it.

Launching himself at her, he used his weight and mass to take her to the floor.

She was a Tasmanian devil under him. She'd once told him hypnosis, like certain drugs, could make a person stronger and more agile. They didn't feel pain.

Stronger was a definite. Even though he outweighed her by at least fifty pounds, she rolled them both over and pushed herself away from his grip. Snagging a book off the table near Lippenstein's recliner, she swung it at his head.

He blocked it and knocked the volume away, mentally scrambling for something else to ask Spear, to keep him talking. "Why make yourself look like me?"

The mastermind enjoyed proving his intellect. "Similar features and build. I'd already picked you out from the endless stream of men and women going to and from her office before I even realized she was in love with you. I took a tactic from her playbook—I created a very realistic mask that made me truly your identical twin."

Vivi broke from Ian's grip and lunged for the stunner. He snagged her around the waist and hauled her back to pin her against the built-in shelves. "Come on, Vivi," he ground out under his breath while staring into her eyes. "Remember me." To their attacker, he yelled, "You're the one who put that photo on her desk that day. You disguised yourself as me to get inside the building past her assistant. Fake pass, too?"

"Trust me, I'm superior to both of you in many, many ways. That's the tip of the iceberg."

Ian wanted to break every bone in Spear's body and strip that puffed up, self-congratulatory tone from his voice. "If you're so goddamn smart, why are you still here? You're about to be surrounded."

"How will they know who the real Ian Kincaid is?" the man taunted.

"Because I'm in communication with them, asshole."

"Not for long," his twin said.

A high-pitched squeal ricocheted through Ian's ear

like an ice pick to his brain. He winced and yanked out the earbud.

Fuck. What had the guy just used? Some type of handheld EMP device?

The unit was dead. With Ian reeling, Vivi broke from his hold. He tripped her, sending her to the floor, then dropped to grab her ankle. She hissed, kicking at his face.

He held on. "Vivi, damn it. Fight this. Fight for us! Wake the fuck up!"

She cursed and continued to drive her feet at him. He knocked one away, grabbed the other, but still earned a boot heel to the nose.

"Time's running out, little bird," the bastard called to her. "Hurry, Genevieve. *Come to me.*"

Fucking asshole. Ear still ringing and nose now bleeding, Ian managed to descend on her once more. Her breath whooshed out on impact, yet she swung a fist, connecting with his temple.

Damn, his wife was a hellion. He grabbed her face with both hands and forced her vacant eyes to focus on him, even as she boxed his ears. "I'm right here. Snap out of it. Come back to me." He realized his mistake. "Come to *me,*" he rephrased, "*little bird.*"

She blinked. Looked at him like she actually saw him. "Ian?"

The bullet hit him in the shoulder, tearing through flesh and bone. Recoiling from the blow, he rolled to see the man standing a few feet away, the weapon in his hand pointed at Ian's face.

"I warned you not to interfere." He stretched out a hand. "Come, Genevieve."

Her gaze went from Ian to his double. She smiled at the man and Ian yelled, "No!" when she reached to take it.

But his wife was under no manipulation anymore, although she seemed to act like it. As the fucker pulled the trigger, she launched herself at him.

―――――――――

THE BULLET HIT her in the chest, the force knocking her on her ass. She was falling...

There were two Ians. The one who stood over her and the other who lay on the floor a foot away. That one roared as warm blood spread over her left side, trickling down her ribcage.

The room swam as the two of them fought, the shadows beginning to close in around her. Her vision narrowed to a pinprick. Her breathing became stilted. She heard another gunshot, but it sounded far away. There was a howl of pain, fists hitting flesh and the crashing of bodies into furniture.

She was floating, pain lancing through her chest, up into her collarbone. Glancing across the way, she saw Dr. Lippenstein lying on the floor. His blank stare told her he was...

No, couldn't be. What had happened? Where was Ian? *Her* Ian?

Stars danced at the edges of her perceptive field. Her chest felt so heavy, clogged, as if she were trying to breathe under water. Strangled sounds came from her mouth.

The fighting men drew close; one tripped over her leg. She barely felt it, her limbs numb.

"Stay with me," she heard Ian shout and she knew he was speaking to her, but she was so tired. *Just need to close my eyes for a minute.*

A thick-soled boot stepped on her hand, jerking her back to consciousness. It wasn't Ian...

It was the other man. The one who looked like her husband but wasn't.

Memories flooded back to her. Of this place, of her mentor.

Of her dad.

My little bird, he'd always called her. Her eyes teared. It was the reason she'd had such a fondness for them.

He would have liked Ian, she thought dreamily. Her breathing was shallow, there was only the tiniest tunnel of light in her eyes, showing her the tin ceiling high above.

"Ian?" Her voice came out bubbly. She coughed.

"Fight, Vivi!"

Inside her mind palace, she saw the two of them married, living in a cute house with two kids. They were laughing.

There was a grunt, a kick to her side. Pain flared icy hot slapping away the fantasy. A heavy weight fell on her stomach.

The imposter had dropped his gun. The shiny metal caught her focus, made the shadows recede. Or maybe it was the searing heat in her chest that now seemed unbearable.

She couldn't lose him.

Save Ian.

Blinking, she raised the gun with wobbling hands and tried to focus. Fired.

One of the men collapsed next to her, his face frozen in shock. His eyes...

Vivi sucked in a breath. What had she done?

"Vivi." The body was jerked away, the other man dropping to his knees beside her, holding his shoulder.

His face was a mess, blood running from his nose, an eye swelling. He tugged the weapon from her grip and tossed it across the room, his upper body bowing over her.

The shadows began closing in again, the floating feeling returning. She tried to hang on, to look into his gaze one last time. She had to be sure.

He pressed his hands against her wound. "Don't you even think about dying on me, you hear? Don't you fucking leave me, Vivi."

She couldn't see his eyes. "Ian?" she choked out. "Is that you?"

His gaze flew to hers. "It's me," he said. "You're going to be all right."

Pine green. His eyes were the right color.

The sound of others entering the house echoed around her. Vivi tried to reach up and touch his face, but her strength was gone. "I saved you," she whispered.

That was all that mattered.

His eyes were the last thing she saw before the shadows took over.

TWENTY-THREE

F *our days later*

THE BULLET HAD MISSED her heart by centimeters. Ian had nearly died himself when he'd seen her fall.

She'd spent several days in intensive care, him hovering over her, his own wounds treated and healing.

Spear was on a ventilator, not expected to live. During the fight, Vivi's wire had caught his confession.

Ian had sat faithfully next to his wife's bed, waiting for her to wake. He'd been ready to take out any threat that walked through the door of her room, be it Command & Control, Homeland, or the fucking President himself.

Although he'd defied Beatrice's orders, he had yet to answer for it. While he was at the hospital, guarding Vivi, his boss had taken the recording and went to someone—he didn't know who—and cleared Vivi's name. The U.S. government had reinstated her as a living, breathing patriot.

His wife, a bloody hero.

Said hero was writing in her notebook as she defied doctor's orders and prepared to go home—which, for now was SFI Headquarters. He had plans to change that very soon, but for the moment, they were safest there. They both needed to heal, to rest, to simply have time together.

She finished off the message she'd insisted he deliver and tore the paper from the rings. "Tell him I'm sorry I can't stay until he's released."

Using a single hand, since his left arm was in a sling, Ian maneuvered the wheelchair next to the bed. "Tell him yourself."

Frowning, she allowed him to help her off the mattress, but resisted sitting. "I'm perfectly capable of walking out of here on my own two feet."

"Doctor's orders," he replied, "and if you don't obey, I'll be forced to sic Beatrice on you."

Narrowing her eyes, but also teetering a bit because she wasn't yet as strong as she claimed, she glared at him. "That's low."

He smiled. "If I have to force you to take care of yourself, I will use all the tools in my arsenal to do so." When she stepped toward the door, unsteady on her feet, he wanted to shake her. Instead, he said, "Guess I have no choice but to carry you, then."

She let out a whoop when he made to grab her, losing her wobbly balance. Deftly, even with only one good arm, he maneuvered the wheelchair under her before she toppled.

She laughed and the sound was a balm to his heart. "Damn, you're good."

"You suck as a patient, you know."

"So I've been told. At least I don't have a frown carved into my face like that witch of a nurse in intensive care. I swear, some people live to make others miserable and she's one of them."

They'd tried sneaking into Dr. Lippenstein's room to check on him and been promptly dressed down by Nurse Ratched, as Vivi had labeled her.

He grabbed the bag Sabrina had brought to the hospital with a few of Vivi's borrowed clothes and toiletries. "So use your psychobabble on her."

She gave him a look that said she didn't like the term. "Better than holding a gun to her head, I suppose."

Touché. "My methods may differ from yours but are still effective in certain circumstances."

"Agreed. Are you sure Beatrice okayed us returning to headquarters?"

Lawrence's plan had unspooled and the man had been taken into custody by the German government. They were anxious to get Spear, too, but that was doubtful since the guy wasn't expected to survive. Due to the international aspect of the crime, Homeland was in line to prosecute Lawrence as well.

Ian stopped at the door and propped it open, the action taking longer than it should have due to the sling. "I suspect she wants to make us pay for our insubordination, but yeah, she ordered me to bring you home."

"She just wants me to continue my sessions with Sloane."

"That, too."

The floor of the hallway gleamed under the lights. Staff, visitors, and others raced back and forth between rooms. The head nurse came from behind the desk and stopped them, smiling at Vivi and putting a hand on Ian's good arm. "I better not see either of you back any time soon, you hear? Want me to walk you to the exit?"

Vivi smiled. "Not necessary, but thank you."

"Here are your discharge papers. I'm surprised he got you in that chair."

Ian grinned. "I have my ways."

Vivi smacked him with the folded papers.

The woman winked and lowered her voice. "Your sexy bodyguard wouldn't let me touch that wheelchair even if I wanted to. He's a keeper. Take your meds and get some rest. Let him save the world next time."

Ian chuckled. "There is one thing you could do for us," he said.

"What's that, Sugar?"

As if Vivi caught his train of thought, she nodded. "I want to say goodbye to my mentor. He's still in guarded condition but is awake. The ICU nurse, however, has forbid me from coming within a hundred yards of his room."

A wave of her hand. "Oh, Sheila gets real protective of her patients. I'll call down there and see what I can do."

Sure enough, when they arrived at the intensive care unit, Sheila was on the phone with her back to the patient hallway. Ian practically sprinted past the desk, leaning low over Vivi and making her giggle as he raced them to Lippenstein's room.

Inside, the curtains were drawn, the space dark. A monitor beeped in a steady rhythm next to the bed.

"Thank God," the man said. "They're going to kill me in here."

Ian shut the door behind them before starting to wheel Vivi closer. She held up a hand to stop him, then shoved herself to her feet and walked to her mentor's bedside. "They're taking excellent care of you and you better not give them any grief." She took his hand as Ian turned on a light. "I need you. Promise me you'll do as the doctor says and take care of yourself."

"That's right." Lippenstein scratched at the covers over his belly. Ian suspected he was bandaged up good after his surgery to remove the bullet and repair his abdomen. "We have a session to finish, don't we?"

Vivi smiled but Ian caught the way she paled at the idea of undergoing hypnosis again. He couldn't blame her. "I'm holding you to it," she said, leaning over and kissing the man's forehead.

"Your dad would be proud," Lippenstein said.

Vivi blinked and swallowed but Ian saw the tears in her eyes. "Thank you for being there for him. For me, too."

He patted her hand, sighing. "Get out of here before Nurse Ratched comes in."

"That's exactly what I called her when she chased me off yesterday."

They shared a knowing smile, two colleagues, friends.

After saying their goodbyes, Ian pushed her to the exit. A black SUV idled at the curb, heavy metal music thumping through the tinted windows. "Looks like our ride is here."

Vivi once again thrust herself from the seat, as if she didn't want Beatrice or whoever was inside to see any weakness. "Let me do the talking, okay?"

Not really, but he wasn't going to argue. Not today.

Mick Ranger was in the driver's seat, tapping his thumb to the beat. As Ian helped Vivi into the backseat, he turned down the song and eyed them in the rearview behind his dark sunglasses. "Hey, Doc."

"Hi." She offered an appraising glance as Ian climbed in beside her. An orderly rushed out to retrieve the wheelchair. "You're the man who helped me escape prison."

"That's me." He wheeled them away. "Don't make me regret it."

There was no else inside the vehicle. Ian relaxed. He would take Beatrice's wrath like a good soldier and do whatever was necessary to make his wife happy. If she wanted to stay at SFI for a while, he'd stay. If she wanted to leave, they would leave.

"I hear you're a pretty good shrink," Ranger said as he stopped at a red light.

"Don't ever call me that," she replied, flashing a dangerous smile.

The man's return grin acknowledged her wish. "Got any openings Friday? That's my first free day."

For half a second, Vivi said nothing. "I'll check my appointment calendar and get back to you with a time."

Ian let out his breath softly.

A nod and they moved forward again. The divider between the seats went up, giving them privacy. The music volume increased, but was muffled enough they could talk.

"You can't be serious," he said, although he hoped she was. "He's deranged, you know."

"I've seen his file. I know all about his type."

"You do?"

She threaded her fingers through his. "Do you know how many prisons he's escaped from? I want to pick his brain in case I ever find myself in one again."

Ian shook his head, then slid his good arm around her shoulders and pulled her close. "That's my wife."

She kissed him, and although they were both dinged up and sore, he soon had her in his lap. He lost count of the blocks they passed and how much time went by, soaking in her scent and the feel of her under his good hand.

Frustrated and needing to touch her everywhere, he shucked the sling and carefully worked both hands under her blouse and up to her breasts. Avoiding the bandages that covered her wound, he wondered how soon he could get her naked.

They were breathing hard and she was nibbling at his earlobe, whispering her plans for him later that night, when he caught sight of the landscape through the window. At some time during their make-out session, Ranger had driven them out of the city. Blocks of suburbia flew past the window.

He gently shifted Vivi to the seat. "What is he up to?"

She peered out with him. "I thought we were going to SFI."

"Maybe the Queen B changed her mind." The scenery looked familiar, though. "Or maybe..."

"What?"

He grinned. "When she said 'home,' she actually meant *home*."

Vivi gave him a confused glance but within minutes they were pulling into the Reese's drive.

The screen slid down and Ranger asked over the music, "Need help getting inside?"

Ian opened the back door and held out a hand to his wife. "Got it covered."

Ranger tipped a non-existent hat at them. "See you Friday, Doc."

Ian punched in the security code and led Vivi into the foyer. "Welcome to Casa Greene."

There was a moment of silence as she glanced around. "I don't understand."

He tossed his sling on the nearby table and kissed her. She was still weak and when he felt her tremble, he scooped her up like a bride and headed for the bedroom.

They pulled up short when he stepped into the living room and a cheer went up.

Half of Shadow Force was packed into the space like sardines. Every seat was occupied and more folks crowded around the edges. A bird cage hung from a chain screwed into the ceiling. Sherlock and Watson whistled and chirped.

Sloane was in Beatrice's lap on the couch, Cal next to her. They both stood, Beatrice setting Sloane down. "Welcome back," she said as the girl ran to them.

Ian put Vivi on her feet carefully, steadying her as the

girl threw her arms around Vivi's legs. "I missed you," Sloane said, staring up at Vivi with a touch of hero worship in her eyes.

She caressed the girl's hair. "I missed you, too." Glancing around, she gave Beatrice a wary smile. "What is all this?"

Beatrice motioned at Rory, who pushed off the wall where he'd been leaning, crutches supporting him. He walked two feet and tossed a manila folder on the coffee table. "Your name has been cleared. Your passport, driver's license, birth certificate...it's all there. Your bank accounts have been restored and there's an employment offer from NSA."

Her face fell. *"What?"*

"They want you back," Beatrice said, then held up a thin, spiral-bound notebook. "I brought your calendar. Connor's been making appointments. Thought you might want to see how much you're needed at Shadow Force."

"Just to be clear," Rory said, returning to his spot, "*I* don't need therapy. Not your kind, anyway."

The others laughed, yet seemed to hold their breath. Vivi gave the man a skeptical appraisal. "We should talk about that, actually."

Sabrina, wedged between him and Connor, pinched Rory's arm. "Told you so, you old buzzard. Everybody needs therapy."

"I, for one, have qualms about you digging around in my noggin," Zeb said from across the room, "but I'm willing to give it a try if you'll stay, Dr. Montgomery."

Trace spoke up. "If Zeb will do it, that says a lot." He

gave Moe, on the other side of the fireplace mantle, a pointed look. "Some of us need more help than others."

Parker grinned and poked her boyfriend, laughing along with the others. He appeared highly offended. "You're not getting inside my bloody head," he declared to Vivi.

"Honestly, I have no desire to," she countered without missing a beat. "There are some subjects even I can't help."

Jeers and more laughter echoed in the high-ceilinged room. Parker made a sizzling noise and touched his arm as if Vivi had burned him. He screwed up his face and did an exaggerated eye roll.

Ian slid his arm around her, knowing she was out of gas and needed to lie down. He intended to be right there beside her. "She needs to take it easy before she takes on this measly lot." He glanced at his boss. "I assume we can stay for a few days?"

Beatrice nodded and scooped up Sloane when the girl ran back to her. "As long as you need. And no pressure, Vivi, about coming to work for SFI. With your name cleared, you're free to go wherever you want and pursue your dreams."

Placing a hand on his chest, Vivi stared up into Ian's eyes. "My dream is right here. Where Ian goes, I go."

"Aww," Sabrina said.

"If you work for me, he'll be required to as well." Beatrice nodded at Cal for him to explain.

The man crossed his arms. "You're still a potential weapon in the wrong hands, and if you don't work for NSA, they need certain guarantees."

Ian's stomach fell. "Like what?"

"She'll be required to have a bodyguard twenty-four-seven," Beatrice said.

"We just happen to have a new designation for that level of security," Cal added, his chin jutting toward Ian. "You'll need to qualify, of course, to make everyone happy, but—"

"I'll do it," Ian said, cutting him off. "Whatever's required." He looked at Vivi. "That is, if you decide to accept Beatrice's offer."

She worried her bottom lip. "I have a few negotiating points we need to discuss."

"Like not having to listen to Moe bitch and whine," Rory volunteered.

More laughter. Moe made a face. His boss smiled. "We can discuss them first thing in my office tomorrow. Cassandra will have a contract drawn up and papers for you to sign."

"We'll be there," Vivi said, hugging Ian to her. "My bodyguard and me."

Goodbyes were said. Cal lingered a moment behind the rest. "The house is yours to use as long as you like. Consider it a sign-on bonus."

"Stop bribing her," Beatrice called. "It's a wedding gift, Vivi."

Vivi laughed. "Now who's bribing us?"

Soon they were alone. Ian put her to bed, brought the birds in and opened the door to their cage as she requested. Leaving her laughing at their antics, he went to round up food. The stuff in the hospital sucked and he was starving.

When he returned, she was curled into a ball, asleep. The kitchen had been well-stocked and he set the tray with sandwiches and drinks on the nightstand. There were even strawberries, Vivi's favorite. The birds had voluntarily returned to their cage and were both sleeping, too.

Eating could wait. Trying not to wake her, he carefully crawled in next to her.

Sighing, she tucked herself against him. "Thank you," she said, sleepily. "For everything."

He held her close. "No thanks needed. You're all I want, Genevieve Montgomery."

She pushed slowly up onto her elbow and stared down into his face. "That's Montgomery-Kincaid, I'll have you know."

Slipping his hand to the back of her head, he gently guided her in for a kiss.

It turned hotter, more demanding, but when she grimaced a moment later, he stopped. "You need to eat."

She sighed. "And take a bath."

"I can help with that." He gave her a disarming grin. "I'm quite good at underwater techniques."

She laughed. "And since you're going to be my round-the-clock bodyguard"—she batted her lashes—"I must train you to meet my every wish."

He waggled his brows. "Sounds like strenuous work."

"I'm very demanding."

His grin broadened and he stroked her back. "I can hardly wait."

She pointed at the tray. "Care to feed me?"

He sat them both up slowly and snagged a strawberry.

Brushing the fruit over her lips, he nearly moaned when her tongue came out to taste it. "I think you've hypnotized me," he teased, then made a face. "Too soon?"

She playfully punched his belly. "I have a lot to process but Dr. Lippenstein will help, once he's back on his feet. I'm not happy about what took place, but I'm not going to live scared of being used and manipulated again. It won't happen because I have you by my side. Now, feed me, husband."

He held out the strawberry. "Gladly, wife."

She ate everything on the tray he'd brought for her and half of his sandwich, as well. When they finished, he bathed her, careful of her bandages and then tucked her under the covers.

As she spooned against him, he stared at the ceiling and thought about the future. A week ago, he hadn't had one. Had wanted to die because he'd erroneously believed he'd killed the woman next to him.

How things had changed. He now had all he'd ever wanted, and it was because of the same woman. Tugging her closer and enjoying the way she sighed contentedly, he closed his eyes.

He finally had a family. Vivi. SFI. A real, honest-to-god family. Life was better than good and he planned to enjoy every moment of it.

BE sure to catch up with the SEALs and the Spy Division, available at all retailers. And watch for *Covert Tactics*, featuring Rory and Amelia, coming spring 2023!

PNR & UF BY MISTY / NYX HALLIWELL

Paranormal Urban Fantasy:

The Accidental Reaper Series

Grim & Bare It

Killin' It (short story for newsletter subscribers only)

Reaper's Keepers

In too Reap

The Vampire's Kiss (an exclusive short story available ONLY at Misty's Store. *Intended for mature audiences* 17+)

Grave Girl (January 2023)

The Kali Sweet Series

Revenge Is Sweet, Kali Sweet Urban Fantasy Series, Book 1

Sweet Chaos, Kali Sweet Urban Fantasy Series, Book 2

Sweet Soldier, Kali Sweet Urban Fantasy Series, Book 3

Sweet Curse, Kali Sweet Urban Fantasy Series, Book 4

Paranormal Contemporary Romance:

Witches Anonymous Step 1

Jingle Hells, WA Step 2

Wicked Souls, WA Step 3

Dark Moon Lilith, Witches Anonymous Step 4

Dancing With the Devil, Witches Anonymous Step 5

Devil's Due, Witches Anonymous Step 6

Dirty Deeds, Witches Anonymous Step 7

Wicked Wedding, Witches Anonymous Step 8

Paranormal Romantic Suspense:

Soul Survivor, Moon Water Series, Book 1

Soul Protector, Moon Water Series, Book 2

Cozy Mysteries (writing as Nyx Halliwell):

Sister Witches Of Raven Falls Mystery Series

Sister Witches of Raven Falls Special Collection

Of Potions and Portents

Of Curses and Charms

Of Stars and Spells

Of Spirits and Superstition

Confessions of a Closet Medium Cozy Mystery Series

Confessions of a Closet Medium Special Collection

Pumpkins & Poltergeists

Magic & Mistletoe

Hearts & Haunts

Vows & Vengeance

Cupcakes & Corpses

Tea Leaves & Troubled Spirits

Sister Witches of Story Cove (Formerly Once Upon a Witch) Cozy Mystery Series

Cinder

Belle

Snow

Ruby

Zelle

MEET MISTY

USA TODAY Bestselling Author Misty Evans has published over eighty novels and writes romantic suspense, urban fantasy, and paranormal romance. Under her pen name, Nyx Halliwell, she also writes cozy paranormal mysteries.

When not reading or writing, she embraces her inner gypsy and loves music, movies, and hanging out with her husband, twin sons, and three spoiled puppies. She's a crafter at heart and has far too many projects to finish.

Don't want to miss a single adventure? Visit www.mistyevansbooks.com to find out ALL the news!

LETTER FROM MISTY

Hello Beautiful Reader!

Thank you for reading this story! It is an honor and a privilege to write stories for you. I'm an indie author and every fan is important to me. I pour my heart into each story and do my best to bring you an escape from the real world.

I hope you enjoyed this one, and I'd like to ask a favor – would you mind leaving a review at your favorite retailer? Or share your enjoyment of it with a friend or family member? I'd really appreciate it, and reviews help other readers find books they will love too.

Readers are the key to my success - not a traditional publishing deal (had one), an agent (had two), or a publicity team (yep, you guessed it, had one of those as well.)

Those of you who love my characters and worlds, and

who then tell others, are like the very best of friends. I adore you and will keep writing if you keep reading!

If you'd like to learn about my other books, sales, and special promotions, please sign up for my newsletter at **www.mistyevansbooks.com**. You'll get coupons to download starter packs for FREE, whether you love my romantic suspense book or my paranormal. I also have a spy quiz and printable book list you can download.

Support me directly (no retailer taking their cut), grab special edition box sets, and get new releases before they are out at retailers by visiting my store **https://mistye vansbooks.com/shop**. I have sales and offer NEW RELEASES early and at a discount!! Check it out.

Last but not least, if you enjoy clean, cozy mysteries, visit my pen name **www.nyxhalliwell.com** to see those books!

Thank you and happy reading!

Misty

CPSIA information can be obtained
at www.ICGtesting.com
Printed in the USA
LVHW022114080323
741235LV00011B/273

9 781948 686778